"Why didn't you go for the blanket?"

Between acute embarrassment and chattering teeth, George found it difficult to find her voice. Her unscheduled dip in the sea had rendered her thin muslin gown and the gauzy chemise underneath transparent.

As if it were an effort to speak while he looked at her, the viscount cleared his throat and turned his face towards the sea. "If I had gone up to the house and demanded a blanket, then everyone would know I had seen you...like this."

"How very thoughtful you are, Tony!" Disregarding her misery, George attempted to smile.

Lord Sarre turned to look at her again. "George, my dear girl, you may not realize this, but though it was only an accident, this situation could easily be perceived as compromising to your honour. There are those who would insist I marry you at once."

George's mouth fell open in shock and alarm. "Oh, no, Tony. No, it can't be like that! I won't...I can't...."

He did not allow her to see the flicker of hurt that flit across his features. Instead, he leaned forward to touch her hand in a reassuring gesture, smiled weakly and said, "Never fear, my girl. It shall always be our secret."

AN INFAMOUS SEA BATH

EMILY DALTON

Harlequin Books

TORONTO • NEW YORK • LONDON
AMSTERDAM • PARIS • SYDNEY • HAMBURG
STOCKHOLM • ATHENS • TOKYO • MILAN

Dedicated in memory
of my father, Gerald V. Ford.
I love you, Dad.

"Then all with ails in heart or lungs,
In liver or in spine,
Rushed coastwise to be cured like tongues,
By dipping into brine."
—From the book, *Seaside England*
by Ruth Manning Sanders

Published February 1991

ISBN 0-373-31144-3

AN INFAMOUS SEA BATH

CHAPTER ONE

THEIR MOTHER HAD GIVEN both her older sister and herself rather imposing names; only her sister quite lived up to hers, both in height and queenly bearing, while she did not. No one ever presumed to call Miss Isabella Marguerite Lacy "Bella" or "Margie," for she would have looked down her nose at them with such blistering scorn as to turn them quite pale and speechless. But Miss Georgiana Feona Lacy was known to all and sundry as merely "George."

The name suited her. George was unpretentious, outspoken and friendly to a fault, or so her mother frequently informed her. Her father, however, in a rare expression of opinion, once diffidently observed that George's open manner was refreshing compared to Isabella's, which was haughty and affected. He never repeated the observation, though, since Isabella was quite her mother's "darling own."

"Oh, do take that offensive animal out of the house, George," her elder sister was admonishing her now. "It smells abominably!"

"Pooh, Isabella! Whiskers had a bath not above a fortnight ago. He cannot smell *too* awfully bad!"

"But I say he does! If you do not take that grubby cur outside immediately I shall summon Mama. She will lock your precious Whiskers in the cellar if you do not comply! I begin to feel sick, and if my spirits or my looks are the least damaged by the foul air I am presently breathing you shall have reason to repine!"

George was frequently diverted by her sister's sense of grandeur, but today it was inconvenient to pander to her. They sat in the drawing-room and George had just stretched out on the Chippendale sofa using Whiskers as a cushion at her feet. She was very comfortable and did not wish to rise for any reason.

"Aren't you going into town to shop for some new gloves for the assembly tomorrow night, Isabella? Hadn't you better get ready?" George asked her, hoping to divert her sister's thoughts away from the imagined pollution of the air.

"Well, and I am ready! If you had but looked at me, you should see it is so! Do I usually wear a bonnet to sit indoors of an afternoon, little sister? Hardly!"

George, who was not deficient in understanding, had certainly noticed that Isabella was dressed for a trip into town. She was looking beautiful, as always. The pink muslin day dress and white poke bonnet with a pink feather and trim were not only functional for such a warm June afternoon, but also brought the ivory colour of Isabella's complexion into striking contrast with her chestnut hair. But George was not moved by envy as she surveyed her sister's considerable assets. Since Isabella did not add to these outward attractions strength of character, an improved mind, or even a soft, sweet dash of sentimentality, her beauty was literally skin deep.

"Isn't that Lord Somebody-or-other you're always prattling on about going to be at the Upper Rooms tomorrow, Isabella?" George persisted, determined to keep Whiskers at her feet.

"Do you mean Anthony, Lord Sarre?" her sister enquired coolly and with an exaggerated air of nonchalance.

"If he is the rich viscount on holiday in Bath whom you and Mama have been continually scheming to catch these last two weeks, I suppose so."

"George, must you be so vulgar?" observed Isabella with a disdainful glance at her younger sister's reclining form. "You know nothing about gentlemen or the delicate art of attracting them, so I would keep my low opinions to myself if I were you."

George's reaction to her sister's scathing set-down was a look of wide-eyed innocence and a shrug of her shoulders. Then, since the mention of Isabella's latest matrimonial target had done the trick of getting her mind off of Whiskers's offensive aroma, she picked up a novel, *Sense and Sensibility* written by "a lady" and obtained from the subscription library, and began to read. George soon became absorbed in the story, her blond curls, which were kept relatively short to lessen the ordeal of taming them into neatness, tumbling round her face as she thrust her nose as close to the page as possible.

"George, do sit by the window!" scolded her mother, the Honourable Mrs. Henry George Lacy, as she entered the drawing-room. "Reading in insufficient light will make you as near-sighted as your father, so unless you wish to begin wearing spectacles at an early age, my gel, I suggest that you sit by the window or get a candle."

Mrs. Lacy was a handsome woman, tall, full-figured, and with only a trace of grey showing in her dark hair. She had been as beautiful as Isabella in her youth, but had been dowerless and therefore compelled to be content with marriage to a man who was rich but untitled. She was determined that Isabella would do better. Ambition and avarice had sharpened her features over the years, and she had a hard, piercing eye. She levelled her stern gaze on her younger daughter now.

"George, are you listening to me?"

"Yes, Mama," was George's absent-minded reply as she threw a cushion on the floor in front of one of the windows and proceeded to plump it into a comfortable shape. Then she lay down on the carpet, propped her elbow on the cushion and resumed her reading as before. Whiskers, after circling a chosen area for some time, eased himself down and laid his chin on one of her stockinged feet.

"Oh, Mama, how can you let George behave like such an urchin, lying about in that dowdy old dress, with no shoes and her hair flying untidily about her face? If Lord Sarre continues to show an interest in me, he will soon be calling on us. I hope you will not permit me to be mortified by George's appearance or behaviour!''

"Calm yourself, angel," Mrs. Lacy replied soothingly, as she pulled on her gloves. "You know how tiresome it is to prod George into respectability. I find I have energy enough to do it only when it is absolutely necessary. If, or rather *when,* Lord Sarre calls on us, rest easy that your sister will not shame you! She can look well enough when she is made to.''

George showed no indication by movement or sound that she had heard her mother and sister discussing her. If truth be told, she seldom really listened to their conversations, whatever the subject. Their chief topics of interest were clothes, gossip and romantic strategies, all shallow trivialities as far as George was concerned.

"George, mind you remember to be here to pour your father's tea this afternoon. You know he will forget to drink it entirely if someone is not present to remind him he is thirsty! And I do not want to discover that you have been rambling about the countryside again with that scruffy dog for hours on end! The sun is so injurious to one's skin.''

"She is freckled beyond anything, Mama! I should be mortified if my complexion were half so coarse...." Isabella's querulous voice faded away to a muffled natter as the footman closed the doors behind them and they descended the steps of Lacy Manor to the waiting carriage.

George immediately threw down her book and stood up, gazing through the glass to watch the carriage drive off. "Well, Whiskers," she informed her hairy companion with a satisfied smile, "they're gone at last!" She stooped down and gave the scraggly, black and grey-peppered mutt a squeeze around the neck and pushed the small dog's tangled hair out of its eyes. "Are you ready for a run by the stream?" The dog replied with a sound that was something between a high-pitched bark and an ear-splitting howl and jumped as high in the air as its short, stubby legs would allow. George laughed delightedly.

"Oh, you are an odd mix of low breeding, to be sure, just as Isabella is so fond of telling me! But I find your company preferable to most of the pompous, stiff-rumped people round here, Whiskers!"

They'd started for the door when George remembered that she ought to take her parasol or at least wear a bonnet. But that would mean returning to her bedchamber, and there was the possibility of encountering her mother's nosy abigail or some other officious servant. They would duly note the time of her departure and report it to Mrs. Lacy.

She moved to the Venetian mirror over the fireplace to search her face for the excess of freckles her sister had referred to earlier, and could only detect a faint sprinkling over the bridge of her nose. Otherwise, though her skin was rather more rosy than in the winter months, she saw no reason to suppose that she was turning into a prune. Isabella was more likely to resemble that wrinkled fruit as she aged, thought George with amusement, since her face was so frequently puckered into squeamish lines of disapproval. She smiled then, visualizing her sister's consternation if she could have known her thoughts, and small, even white teeth gleamed between full, pink lips.

She opened the door to the drawing-room stealthily and peeked around the corner. The footman had deserted the entry hall since the mistress and her elder daughter had left and would not be returning for several hours. This was the moment to escape, and George picked Whiskers up and bolted out the door, hugging the cool stone walls of the building until she'd reached the edge of the sloping eastern grounds. Knowing that now she had only to walk a few yards away from the house to be immersed in the cool closeness of the woods, she heaved a relieved sigh and put Whiskers on the ground. Together they entered the tangled green forest that had become a kind of paradise to George.

Warming shafts of sunlight penetrated the leafy maze, turning George's mop of natural curls into spun silver and gold. She picked up sticks as she moved through the trees, throwing them for Whiskers to retrieve as they both dodged moss-covered rocks and gnarled roots writhing above the rich dirt to catch a sunbeam.

When they reached the stream, Whiskers immediately started barking and nipping at George's feet, urging her to run with him. But now that she was here, the idea of a run did not suit George. The sun sparkling on the languid water made her eyelids droop, and she realized that there was nothing she would rather do than take a nap. Turning and discovering a sunwarmed patch of grass near the trunk of a tree, George settled herself upon the fragrant green blades, curled into a ball with her fists nestled beneath her chin, and went to sleep.

"WHAT DO YOU THINK IT IS, my scraggly little friend? A faerie? An elf? Possibly a nymph, though I doubt I should be so lucky! Of the three magical creatures, the nymph would probably object least to a stolen kiss or embrace, don't you think?"

George's eyelids fluttered open at the sound of a man's deep, throaty voice. She no longer lay on her side, but was stretched out on her back in a most unladylike fashion with one leg thrown out to her side, the ruffle of her hem lying just above her knee.

Blinking several times, she was able to discern through sleep-clouded eyes a tall form towering above her. From her perspective on the ground, this giant of a man was all legs, his powerful thighs tightly swathed in buckskin breeches and brilliant boots as tall as church spires. At the very top of this imposing Goliath was dark, wind-tousled hair wreathed in an aureola of light which threw his face into mysterious shadow.

"It wakes, my friend. It moves, but it is not afraid," the voice continued in a lilting, teasing whisper.

Endeavouring to shake off the last remnants of sleep, George sat up and pulled her skirt down about her ankles. The stranger had shifted his head slightly to the right and now the full force of the sun glared down on her, making it utterly impossible to focus on her unexpected visitor. Suddenly George heard Whiskers bark and realized that the "friend" spoken to by the faceless, mesmeric voice was her very own Whiskers. There he sat, just behind the man, happily wagging his tail.

"Please, sir," George implored groggily, extending a slender arm towards the shadowed form above her, "help me rise. I cannot see you from here and it puts me at quite a disadvantage, you know."

"Indeed!" was the forceful reply, as George found her small fingers enfolded in a warm, strong masculine grip. "That is putting it mildly, child."

As George staggered to her full five feet three inches, she realized that, though the man was well above the average in height, he was not the giant she had imagined. He was dressed in a white shirt which was open at the throat, displaying fine black tendrils of hair peeking out at the top. George observed these curious decorations with interest, because since she had no brothers and her father was an extremely modest man, she had never before seen a man's bare chest.

When her gaze finally lifted to the gentleman's face, she discovered him to be clearly amused. Laughing eyes, laced all round with thick, black lashes, slanted downwards into smiling crescents of green. The cheek bones were high and aristocratic, the nose straight and long, the chin a stubborn square with a cleft deeply etched into a faint, dark stubble of beard, the mouth wide and firm, and he was smiling at her.

"Why do you look as though you might eat me?" she burst out without thinking.

The gentleman laughed then, a deep, full-bodied explosion of mirth. "Because you look absolutely delicious, poppet!" he finally said.

"I don't think I understand you, sir," George informed him with a puzzled look. "But I'm quite sure my mother would object to my talking to a stranger thus. Why are you here?" She had not noticed it before, but now she saw that he held a fishing pole in his left hand, and there was a fat, fresh worm tucked snugly on the hook. "You're fishing on my father's land?" She darted him a quick, accusing look. "I should not think he would mind if you had asked permission, sir, but I suspect that you did not ask!"

"On your father's land?" The gentleman's eyebrows lifted as he pointedly surveyed her shabby clothing.

George understood his sceptical scrutiny and blushed. She put her hands on her hips and retorted,

"Yes, on my father's land! I am Miss Georgiana Feona Lacy, if you please!"

"Or one of Miss Georgiana Feona Lacy's servants, I rather suspect." He rubbed his chin consideringly. "If you were an abigail you'd be dressed a little better, though. And you're too refined for a chambermaid, and much too young and pretty for a governess. What a puzzle, what a puzzle..." Suddenly his brow cleared. "Ah, then perhaps you are an elf or a faerie. Or—" and here he grinned "—maybe you're a nymph, after all."

"I can't imagine why you persist in talking fustian, sir!" George exclaimed with a stamp of her foot. "I'm exactly who I say I am! And I demand to know what you're doing on my father's land."

"Well, poppet, if you insist on playing this little game, I shall indulge you," the man conceded with a wink as he settled himself on a large, flat rock by the tree. "I wasn't aware that I was on Mr. Lacy's—your father's—land. I'm visiting Mr. Micah Shelby on the neighbouring estate for a bit of fishing and tea, though my host seems more inclined for tea because he's already given up on catching anything and has gone back to the house. I was wandering down the stream in an effort to find a better spot to throw out my line. Evidently I ventured too far." He bowed slightly from the waist and pursed his lips mockingly, his green eyes dancing all the while with suppressed mirth. "I beg you, forgive me."

"I'm well aware you're playing a farce with me, sir," George returned in a frigid little voice. "But if you're truly visiting Micah, he will tell you exactly who I am. We used to be playmates! Would you like to go up to see him now? I'm ready if you are."

The gentleman had been unwinding his line, but stopped when George finished speaking. He levelled a keen gaze at her and once again looked her over quite thoroughly. All the while George stood with her chin up and her fists resting defiantly on her small hips. Finally his eyes lifted to her own narrowed blue ones and remained there, steady and unflinching.

She had stared down Miss Penelope Farnsworth just last Tuesday when that silly, pudding-faced girl had been so rude as to call her a "hoyden," and George did not see why this gentleman (great, tall man that he was!) should be any different. Several seconds passed and neither pair of eyelids flickered in the least.

Out of the corner of her eye, George could see Whiskers lifting one paw and then the other in a show of nervousness. She endeavoured to ignore him. Then he began whimpering and pressing his wet nose against one of her ankles. The gentleman smiled and so did George, but neither blinked or looked away. But when Whiskers sat up on his hind legs and yelped, George could stand it no longer. Throwing a hand over her mouth to try to prevent a large, unladylike guffaw from escaping, she doubled over and laughed until her sides ached.

"I knew you couldn't do it!" shouted the gentleman triumphantly, slapping his knee and grinning broadly. "My brother always said that I was not to be bested in a staring competition. But you did very well!"

"If not for this silly animal of mine, I should have been able to beat you soundly!" insisted George, catching her breath. "Our stand-off must have made him feel rather fidgety, you know. I imagine we looked like great stags in the forest about to tangle our horns!"

"An interesting comparison, poppet," replied the gentleman with a devilish gleam in his eyes. "But I could never think of you as anything remotely masculine, and you must acknowledge that stags, being the great and glorious stallions of the forest that they are, aren't in the least feminine. But you may compare *me* to a stag whenever you wish!"

George did not quite know how to respond to this little speech, offered with a wry smile and flashing green eyes. But she did know that it made her exceedingly uncomfortable. She felt a moment's panic. He must have sensed her change of mood, because he stood up and smiled kindly, those irrepressible, laughing eyes politely subdued into a more respectful expression.

"How do you do, Miss Georgiana Feona Lacy?" he said, reaching for her hand and bowing gracefully over it. "Forgive me for doubting your identity!"

George's fears vanished under the influence of such a pleasant smile and gentlemanly apology.

"Well, and I do understand your doubts, sir," she admitted graciously, unconsciously picking at the frayed ruffle round her sleeve. "Though Mama has had some nice little gowns made up for me, I cannot see the sense of wearing them when I ramble by the stream or lounge about the house. She insists that I haven't the proper feelings of a young lady, though, or I would always wish to look nice." George sighed heavily. "But she will not suffer me to have my way much longer, I'm afraid."

"And why is that?" enquired the gentleman with an air of friendly interest.

"Since I shall be eighteen in one month's time, she says I must be 'out' at last. She has not hurried the business before, you see, because my elder sister, Isabella..."

"Miss Isabella Lacy is your sister?" The gentleman's eyebrows lifted in surprise.

"You are acquainted with Isabella?"

"I've met her...once or twice at the Bath assemblies," the gentleman replied, turning away and walking to the edge of the stream to sit on the grass. "I thought perhaps you were cousins or something of that nature. You do not resemble each other in looks or manner."

"That observation is brought to my attention on rather a regular basis, sir," George admitted with a chuckle, following him to the stream. "She looks like

Mama, while I take after my father's side of the family! But you needn't pity me, because I would rather not be as beautiful or as tall or as fastidious as Isabella for all the world! I don't think she has much fun, always worrying about her complexion and such. And Mama never leaves her alone,'' she added confidingly, seating herself beside him on the grass, with Whiskers settling himself between them for a nap. "Mama thinks that Isabella's great beauty is destined to shine at some marquis's banquet table, or in some duke's grand salon. And it could not hurt if he were very, very rich!''

The gentleman threw out his line while George watched with interest, quite at her ease. Then he said, "And even though Isabella is not married yet, your mother has decided to bring you out into Society next month?''

"I suppose she cannot keep me tucked away forever, though I would not mind it in the least, since marriage is the furthest thought from my mind! And *that,* I gather, is the purpose of bringing one out. Besides, I think Isabella may have found another suitor to aim for, a Lord Somebody-or-other. I can never remember his name! Always in the past there has been something wrong with the fellow. He is either not titled or not rich, so Isabella will not have him; or he is both titled and rich and he will not have *her!* It has been a vexatious business for my mother, I assure you. But some day I suppose she will dispose of Isabella to some luckless fellow!''

"You do not speak very affectionately of your sister," the gentleman observed, looking teasingly at her from out of the corner of his eye.

"Oh, I suppose I do not!" George exclaimed, blushing hotly. "I beg your pardon! You seem to induce me to speak my mind, however disagreeable its contents! I do love Isabella! I do! Only..."

"Yes?"

"Only I...I sometimes feel she's rather a shallow person."

"How very interesting," the gentleman murmured as his eyes rested thoughtfully on his fishing line drifting peacefully over the gentle ripples of the stream.

Suddenly feeling conscience-stricken for omitting to praise her sister in some way, George searched her mind and said, "But she *is* very beautiful. And she did once give me her crimping iron, though I really don't need one with this mess of curls. But she had got a new one, you know, and..."

"Why don't you want to marry?" the gentleman interrupted, fixing her with a sober stare.

George seemed to take the question as seriously as he'd intended it. She tilted her head to the side and considered it at length. Finally she answered, "I don't know! The state of matrimony doesn't seem to be altogether enjoyed by everyone who enters into it, does it? And besides, I don't think I like all the silliness one must endure during courtship. When Jason Bromley—he's a fellow in our parish—got all moony over me last summer, I thought I'd die! It was very disagreeable having him always sitting in my pocket and treating me as if I were some dainty work of porcelain! And once he tried to kiss me," she confided, her eyes opening wide at the horrific memory of it. "Nothing could have been more odious!"

"Tsk, tsk." The gentleman shook his head sympathetically.

"I made up my mind then and there that I would not speak to him again, and I've been as good as my word!" she assured her listener with a decided nod. "Only it is a good thing that Mama didn't know of his foolish fancy, for she would have *made* me marry him. His family is very rich. But nothing would raise my hackles higher than to have some doltish fellow thrust upon me as a husband simply because he is well-breeched!"

"I understand completely," said the gentleman with a smile.

George smiled back, thoroughly delighted in having met someone so in harmony with her own feelings. "Besides, I think having a friend is much, much preferable to having a husband!"

"Might I be your friend?" asked the gentleman.

"I was hoping you would be," replied George happily. "You seem a right enough fellow! But what is your name?"

After a slight hesitation, the gentleman said, "Do you suppose you could just call me 'Tony' for now? I promise to tell you the rest of my name later."

"Well, it is an odd request, to be sure. It hardly seems proper to call you by your Christian name when we've only just met! But I'll do it if you'll call me 'George'!"

"Agreed!" They shook hands over Whiskers, then proceeded to discuss a myriad of topics, just as two friends might, from fishing, to hounds, to weather, to history, and even the war with Napoleon, which had finally concluded the year before at the battle of Waterloo.

After nearly an hour of easy intercourse, flowing smoothly and eagerly from one subject to another, the gentleman drew a breath and said, "Good gad, you are well-informed for one so young! But now I must return to Micah and tea! He'll be wondering..."

"Tea!" George exclaimed and jumped up hurriedly, startling Whiskers out of an interesting dream and into instant readiness for a chase. "Oh, good heavens, what have I been about? It must be four o'clock already! I must leave you at once! My father will need me to pour his tea, you know, and make him drink it! Goodbye, sir! I mean Tony!"

"But when shall I see you again?" the gentleman enquired, standing up and finding she had already run several yards into the woods.

"I don't know!" George shouted back at him and stopped for an instant. "I'm not out yet, you know, so I hardly go anywhere." She hesitated, frowning, while Whiskers ran circles around her. "But I *must* go now or I shall be in great trouble. And I can't very well explain that I was late for tea because I was talking with a strange man by the stream!''

"But I'm not a strange man," corrected the gentleman. "I'm a friend of Micah's!"

"That's no recommendation to *my* mother," said George, laughing. "Goodbye, Tony!"

"Goodbye, George," he called after her as she disappeared into the thick foliage with Whiskers at her heels. "But I shall contrive to see you again, poppet," he added to himself.

CHAPTER TWO

"MICAH SHELBY is coming to dinner? That odious little upstart! How is it that he means to dine with us, pray tell? He *never* comes to dinner! We never invite him!"

Mr. Lacy withstood this assault from his elder daughter with equanimity. He raised his head, the hair sparse and grey, from the perusal of a very large volume, and shrugged his habitually stooped shoulders.

"Well, I'm not precisely sure how it came about, Isabella," was his vague reply, offered with a puzzled, apologetic air. "He interrupted me shortly after tea... I did have tea this afternoon, didn't I, Georgie?"

"Yes indeed, Papa," answered George, who sat next to him on the settee. "And you drank nearly two cups and ate half a cucumber sandwich!"

"Ah, good." Mr. Lacy pushed his sliding spectacles back onto the bridge of his nose and peered nearsightedly at his wife and elder daughter, sitting across the room. "Well, as I was saying, shortly after tea young Shelby was announced at my library door. I was deeply immersed in a book..."

"A most unusual circumstance," murmured Isabella in a sarcastic aside to her mother.

"...and was not in a humour to meet him. But he seemed intent on expressing his sincere regard for my health and that of my entire family. I listened as long as I could, but was irresistibly drawn to the contents of my book, which is the most excellent volume of Roman history I've ever had the pleasure to read! Georgie, did you know that Roman cities were always built near a—"

"Papa, you'd best continue your story before you forget it," George gently prompted him.

"Eh?"

"Micah Shelby."

"Ah, yes. Well, all at once the fellow was taking his leave and saying that he would see me at seven o'clock. When I asked him what for he merely said, 'for dinner, of course!' I must have invited him. There can be no other explanation." Mr. Lacy resumed his reading, leaving his wife and elder daughter to exchange expressions of exasperated resignation.

"Micah Shelby is the most tiresome young man I've ever had the misfortune to meet," lamented Isabella, fanning herself vigorously. "And to have been living next to him my entire lifetime...!"

"You are coming it too strong, Isabella! I can hardly see how Micah's existence can have been such a trial to you," stated George matter-of-factly. "He's been at Oxford these last two years. Even when he happens to be home for a visit, as now, and dares to approach us on the street, you always stare him down as if he were taking the greatest of liberties! And as he always directs his conversation to me or Mama, I fail to understand your poor treatment of the fellow, especially since we all used to play together before he went away to school!''

"George, your concern for Micah is touching to be sure, but so vulgar!"

"Well, you needn't work yourself into a pucker, Isabella. Remember your complexion! You're bound to break out in spots if you persist in hating everyone."

"I do not hate *everyone,* you little ninnyhammer. But Micah is a presumptuous, dandified, *short* little man with no style and no—"

"Money?" suggested George irrepressibly. "More pity to Micah for being second in line for the inheritance and his brother, Tom, so very healthy! He might have secured Miss Isabella Lacy's regard, otherwise!"

"Oh, you little:...!"

"Girls, girls! My nerves! Please!" expostulated Mrs. Lacy. "If I cannot sit quietly in my drawing-room before dinner for even ten minutes without the two of you pecking away at each other like a couple of distempered hens off their lay...!"

Just then the butler appeared at the door.

"Yes, Appleby?" sighed Mrs. Lacy, pressing her two middle fingers against her temples to ease the tension clumping there.

"Mr. Micah Shelby," Appleby intoned.

When Micah entered the room, George could have sworn he'd brought a breath of fresh air with him. Used to Isabella's particular friends (who were nearly as disagreeable as she was) and an odd assortment of gossipy neighbours and seasonal inhabitants of Bath whose importance recommended them to her mother's notice, she found Micah's familiar, boyish face and shock of red hair a welcome sight. But somehow he seemed different tonight. She remembered that as a boy he'd exhibited a tendency to blink when he was nervous. He was blinking excessively now.

"Mr. Lacy, Mrs. Lacy, Miss Lacy... George! How do you do! How do you do! Such a pleasure to see you! I was telling m'father just t'other day that I haven't been so fortunate as to dine with the Lacys in an age! Dash it all, never a good idea to neglect one's neighbours, y'know!"

Micah had seated himself in the chair closest to George and looked about as comfortable as a fox in a kennel of slavering hounds. His neckcloth, a fine, complicated creation of tucks and twists, looked to be choking him, for his face was as bright and red as a spring poppy and clashed with his purple-striped waistcoat.

"Micah, are you finished at Oxford?" enquired Mrs. Lacy in an attempt at polite conversation.

"Of all the words in the English language, Mrs. Lacy, I must admit that 'finished' is probably the most apt description of my career at Oxford. Ha!" Micah slapped the arm of the brocade winged chair he was occupying, grinned foolishly and blinked thrice.

George couldn't help but giggle, while her mama and Isabella sucked in their cheeks and flared their nostrils most forbiddingly. George's old playmate was acting more freakish than usual, but why he should be so nervous was beyond her. Micah had been exposed to the haughty disdain of her mother and sister, and the complete neglect of her father, since he was in leading strings. Something was afoot.

"I gather you're rusticating for a while, Micah," George offered.

"Yes. M'father don't care if I finish my education. But he says I haven't the wit to run the estate while m'brother Tom's abroad, so I don't know what I'm going to do. I've run through my quarterly allowance already, so there's no use going to Town," Micah candidly revealed. "Hate Bath, y'know. Only good for gouty old men these days. Brighton's the place t'be now. No confounded Master of Ceremonies like Captain Wade to spoil one's fun with a bunch of claptrap about proper dress and decorum! Can get up to any old rig and row there! B'sides, Prinny don't care for Bath and people of fashion ain't to be found there any more."

Micah could hardly hope to endear himself to Mrs. Lacy and Isabella by speaking in such terms, since they both prided themselves upon being members of the first circle of Bath Society. George sighed. If he continued to talk with such ill-advised unrestraint, she could not hope to extricate him from a most uncomfortable evening.

The first two courses at dinner passed in almost complete silence, but George would have as lief done without conversation if Micah persisted in exposing himself as a nitwit. She had been tempted to ask him about Tony, but could not do so in her mother's hearing, for she would have immediately taken George to task for conversing with a man she had not been formally introduced to. She hoped she hadn't seen the last of Tony. Her curiosity was much piqued by him. He was so very *likeable!* He made her laugh, and she loved to laugh.

Later, over a delicious roast of lamb, Micah seemed to shake off whatever had silenced him for a space of time and shocked them all by saying, "I say, isn't George ready to be out? Danged shame she misses all the assemblies and such! Know I'd be devilish glad to face another roomful of turbanned dowagers holding up the walls if only I could depend on seeing George at the Upper Rooms!"

All the ladies stared at Micah, and even Mr. Lacy glanced up from the soup-splattered pages of his Roman history to eye his guest with mild curiosity.

"Mean to say," Micah continued in a great hurry, "wish George were out! There's an assembly tomorrow night, y'know, and...and I'd be happy to engage myself for the first set of dances, if only George...if only George were out!" After this outburst, Micah fixed his rapidly blinking eyes on his

plate and seemed intent on devouring his meat in re-
cord time.

George watched, horrified, as her mother's astonished expression was transformed by sure stages into
greedy speculation. Bringing a glass of wine to her
lips, Mrs. Lacy exchanged a knowing look with her
elder daughter. Mr. Lacy had shrugged and returned
to his book, but George was beyond the power of
movement or speech in any form. If she could have,
she would have screamed! Was this her friend Micah?
Was this her playmate through years of childhood,
running between the hedgerows together and skip-
ping rocks on the pond? How could he have turned so
traitorous as to have begun to think of her as a
woman?

George glanced down at her dress. It was a delicate
shade of misty green, well-fitting and very feminine.
She had chosen it from other less becoming dresses to
please her mother, but obviously it had been a terri-
ble mistake! Somehow it had scrambled Micah's already slightly disordered wits and turned him into an
absolute looby!

"I had planned to bring George out next month
when she turns eighteen," her mother was saying now,
bestowing a benevolent smile upon Micah, the likes of
which he certainly had never seen before. "I wanted
to give her a ball here at the manor, you know, and
invite the best of Bath Society. But I've not been absolutely set on such a plan. I can see your point of view

as well. 'Why wait?' you say. And somehow I think I begin to agree with you."

Micah didn't look as though he knew how to react to such prompt acquiescence to his way of thinking. He seemed to try to smile, but the result only made one suppose he was feeling more pain than pleasure. "Then I may expect to see George at the assembly tomorrow night?" he choked out between blinks.

"Indeed you may," Mrs. Lacy concurred, smiling graciously.

"Would you like some more lamb, Micah?" purred Isabella.

"IT IS DONE, Tony, and a damned horrid task it was! That woman is the outside of enough! Thought I'd gag on my mutton when she began to ooze approval. I think I'd much rather she continued to hate me than to smirk in that hypocritical way and look me over as if I were the fatted calf! And poor George! Poor, poor George!" Micah groaned and covered his face with his hands, falling into a chair and throwing one leg over the arm of it.

"I greatly appreciate your efforts, Micah!" said Lord Sarre with a satisfied smile. "And the pair of greys will be delivered to your stable within the week!"

Anthony Charles Braithwaite, Lord Sarre, from the county of Gloucester, spruce, freshly shaven and dressed in the uniform black Beau Brummel recommended for evening wear, was pleased that his young friend had pulled it off so admirably. The price, an excellent pair of geldings, was well worth it.

"But how I hate to grieve the child!" Micah groaned through the cracks between his fingers. "We grew up together! Now she looks at me as if I were some kind of toad!" He flung his hands away and grasped the arms of the chair dramatically.

"Rather you than me!" the viscount observed mildly. "Somehow I had to get her circulating, but without showing any interest in her beyond friendship. If she suspects that I'm interested in her as a woman, she'll refuse to speak to me. And how better to impress her mother with the need to introduce her into Society than a possible attachment on your part? Mrs. Lacy may despise you as a neighbour, Micah, or as a suitor for her precious Isabella, but I imagine she thinks you are quite good enough for George! I find it remarkable that Mrs. Lacy has already construed my mild flirtation with Isabella as a desire for imminent marriage!" The viscount frowned and swallowed his last bit of brandy, closing his eyes as the mellow liquid warmed his throat.

"I'm still not convinced I'm doing the right thing, Tony," Micah persisted. "You've got a devilish reputation with the ladies, and George... Well, George isn't like most women! If you hurt her, Tony, I may have to knock you down! It won't be easy, of course, since I do not visit Gentleman Jackson regularly, as you do!"

"Jeopardizing the purity of your profile, my good man, will not be necessary," Lord Sarre assured his friend. "I only mean to get to know her better. I've no intention of sending her into a decline!" The viscount moved to the window and stared into the stark blackness of a moonless night. "Besides, you have the greys to soothe your ruffled composure, Micah. think of them if your conscience keeps you awake tonight." He turned and smiled at his friend, effectively removing the sting from his words.

"Well, I deserve the greys for facing such an evening! And I feel sure I shall be earning the pleasure of owning two such well-matched, sweetgoers for weeks to come!"

"Indeed you may, Micah, for I have plans!"

The viscount's gleaming green eyes sent a shiver of apprehension down Micah's spine. "Good God, Tony, if you hadn't been such a good friend of Tom's, pulled him out of scrapes when you went to school together and all that, and pulled us both out of a scrape or two in Town..."

"A scrape or two...?" Lord Sarre's eyebrows lifted expressively.

"Whatever! Anyhow, if Tom and I didn't owe you for your kind services in the past—the greys be damned!—I'd refuse to take part in this charade!"

"But I've told you, Micah," the viscount returned seriously, "I've no intention of hurting the chit! Have you no faith in me?"

"You refuse to say exactly what you *do* intend, Tony!"

"Simply because I do not know!" the viscount growled impatiently. He took a deep breath, then added in a quieter tone, "I beg your pardon for my waspishness, Micah. If you wish to withdraw your support, do so now and I will think of some other way."

"No, dash it! I'll go along with it, but only as long as I'm sure that George is quite safe from you." Micah looked hard at his companion, but he did not respond. Lord Sarre had turned to stare out the window again and his mouth was set in a straight, stubborn line.

Micah sighed and gave up the conversation. He wasn't one to beat a dead horse. "Well then, don't mean to be rude, Tony, but I'm turning in. M'father's already gone to bed. But perhaps you've changed your mind and will stay the night? I believe I can offer you accommodations as comfortable as your rooms at the Queen's Square."

"No thank you, Micah. I have business in town early in the morning."

"See yourself out then, will you? Devilish fagged! George's dragon of a mother saps me of all my strength! Oh, by the by, they all mean to be at the Pump Room tomorrow at about eleven. I managed to extract Mrs. Lacy's solemn promise that George would be there, and George looked as though she'd like to see *me* carted off to the guillotine!"

The viscount crossed the room and laid his hand on Micah's shoulder, smiling warmly. "You've done very well, my friend! Thank you!"

"Only hope I don't live to regret it," Micah mumbled as he walked away, distractedly ruffling his hair and pulling his Titus style all out of recognition. "See you at the Pump Room then. Good night!"

Lord Sarre watched his young friend exit the room, his firm mouth pursed reflectively. He still held the empty brandy snifter and was rubbing the rim with an idle thumb. He didn't blame Micah for distrusting his intentions towards Georgiana Lacy. He'd never, in his entire experience with women, taken even one of them seriously.

He was twenty-eight years old, the owner of a productive estate his good father had left him on his death five years earlier, and a great disappointment to his grandmother, who had raised him from childhood after the early demise of his mother. Grandmother Braithwaite's dearest wish in the world was for a great-grandchild. And the duty of perpetuating the Braithwaite line might be entirely his own, for the Lord knew his brother might never produce offspring if he did not change his present ways!

The viscount's brow furrowed as he thought about his younger brother, John. He began to pace the floor impatiently.

Yet, why should *he* marry? He was of the same opinion as Miss Lacy where marriage was concerned: few people truly seemed to enjoy it! But then he re-

membered the naive glow of conviction that bright-
ened Georgiana Lacy's eyes when she'd expressed the
thought—quite an original one for an English schoolgirl, he reflected—and how the long, golden eyelashes curled against her cheek when she slept. He
stopped pacing.

God, what a vision she'd been as she lay innocently
immersed in some childish dream! The muslin dress
sprigged with faded daisies and the hem pulled up to
expose one trim ankle and a creamy calf... And that
elfin cap of yellow curls tumbling alluringly onto the
lush, fragrant carpet of grass... Feeling his pulse
quicken at the mere memory of the chit, he walked to
the satinwood table by the settee and poured a small
amount of brandy into the snifter, gulping down the
liquor with a swift tip of his hand.

He knew that Georgiana was somehow different
from all the others, but he wished she weren't. Damn,
he wished she were a servant girl with the mind of a
simpleton, for then he would be immune to her pixie
charms or at least bored with them after a few days.
But this was not the case. This faerie had substance
and seemed to promise a wealth of delight each time
she opened her mouth to express a thought. As the
daughter of an untitled but old and respected family,
permanently ensconced in Bath Society, she was emi-
nently suited to a life of gentility. And though, from
what he'd observed and from all Micah had told him,
her family clearly did not esteem her, to him she was
a diamond of the first water—only a little rough

around the edges. Did he want to smooth those rough edges? he wondered. Only time would tell, he knew, time spent with the girl, talking and delving into that keen little mind of hers. But he found he was not averse to the task. If only he did not have this other worry, and John to think about . . .

Then, reminding himself that he was in Bath on business and not on holiday as everyone supposed, he replaced the snifter on the table and briskly left the room to give orders for his horse to be brought round.

GEORGE DID NOT HAVE an abigail. Her mother had never deemed it necessary. But this morning Isabella's snooty lady's maid woļ e her with the news that she was there by Mrs. Lacy's express wish and was to render her presentable. George knew that this would not be a pleasurable activity for the woman, and felt that the maid's obvious displeasure was some compensation for the fuss and bother she would have to endure herself. But she realized how fruitless it would be to disoblige her mother in this new quirk she had got into her head, because, like a hound on the scent, Mrs. lacy was excited about the possibility that she might, without any effort or the expense of a coming-out ball, dispose of her younger daughter in respectable matrimony.

Micah was preceded in birth by his brother, Tom, but it was inevitable that old Mr. Shelby would use his influence and considerable wealth to establish Micah comfortably in the world. Perhaps he would buy him a living and Micah would become a clergyman. The picture of her childhood friend delivering a sermon would ordinarily have made George laugh, but today her spirits were too downcast to allow for such levity.

George sat in complete dejection of mind as the unsmiling abigail tugged and teased her hair into a stylish cluster of curls at the crown of her head. Then she pulled a few tresses loose and crimped them into tighter curls around her face. Admonishing George to remain seated, Perkins—for that was the abigail's name—then opened the wardrobe and stood considering for a moment before she chose a cornflower-blue walking dress with a matching blue-and-white-striped spencer. She laid the dress on the bed and left the room, returning in a moment with some ribbon that perfectly matched the gown. She then proceeded to wind the silk ribbon round the cluster of curls at George's crown.

George couldn't help but notice that the blue ribbon seemed to bring out the colour of her eyes, and when she had put on the gown and stood surveying herself in the mirror she was aghast to discover the whole effect to be extremely flattering. Even Perkins managed a tight little smile and seemed to be very well pleased with her handiwork.

"Good gad, what's to be done now?" The agitated expression fell from George's lips quite unintentionally, but Perkins was deeply offended.

"Whatever can you mean, miss?" she enquired coldly, the pleased smile entirely vanished from her face. "I'm used to dressing one of the finest, most beautiful young women in the kingdom, and do very well by *her*. Do you mean to imply that you are displeased with your appearance?"

"More than displeased! Dismayed! Depressed! *Horrified!*" George fell slumped into the chair by the dressing table while the abigail went out in a huff, no doubt bending her steps purposefully towards Mrs. Lacy's bedchamber.

This business with Micah! Why he had gotten himself into such a distempered freak was a mystery to George! She had tossed and turned thinking about it all through the long night. She had been very little in Society, and had no real experience with the male sex, but his sudden admiration did not ring true. Her only hope was to somehow withstand her mother's devious machinations to bring about a match and help Micah see that his fancy for her (whether it be real or imagined, or some sort of game) was not bound to bring him joy.

Unaccountably, in the midst of these miserable thoughts, yesterday afternoon's meeting with the gentleman who called himself Tony flashed vividly before her mind's eye. She could almost feel the warm sun beating down on her head and see its beams dancing off the cascading water. But most delightful to remember was the gentleman's infectious laugh and his flashing green eyes. She would like to ask Micah about him, but she was so angry with her old playmate that she didn't know whether she had the patience to speak to him at all!

She heard her mother approaching the door, her full, satin skirts swishing noisily down the hall. George willed strength into her limbs and stood up. She was not in any humour to face down her mother in a shouting competition. She would go to the Pump Room. But she would not behave.

CHAPTER THREE

A STRONG ENGLISH SUN had steamed away the morning mist and now poured its vigorous beams onto the paved promenade of the Royal Crescent. The curved stretch of white stone buildings stood, elegant and immaculate, against a background of verdant countryside. It was a stunning piece of architecture and Lord Sarre, though he had walked the popular promenade time and again, was seeing it with new eyes. The beauty of Bath he had long acknowledged and appreciated, but could it be duplicated on a less grand scale somewhere else? he wondered.

With his hands loosely linked behind a straight, broad-shouldered back, Lord Sarre turned his head slowly to follow the many-windowed, many-columned facade of the structure. His royal-blue coat of Bond superfine followed perfectly the trim line of his athletic physique, and his white pantaloons shaped themselves quite accurately to a fine pair of legs.

The short, slight, middle-aged gentleman who stood beside him, dressed in his habitual uniform of a brown coat and practical brown pantaloons, waited expectantly. When Lord Sarre did not immediately speak,

Mr. Wood could not prevent himself from offering comment.

"The limestone is from local quarries, quite soft when excavated and easily trimmed and molded into whatever shape one might wish." Still no response. "My personal assistant returned from Bleadon only last night to assure me that a quarry dug near the spot you are decided upon would yield the same sort of excellent white stone in abundance. In fact, a project like the one you are considering was started in Bleadon, but abandoned before it was given a good chance."

"Yes, I know," replied the viscount noncommittally. He then proceeded to walk along the promenade, observing the building with a keen, judicious eye. It was too early in the day for much traffic in the area and he was thus spared the necessity of snubbing anyone who might approach him while he was so thoroughly preoccupied. Finally, just as Mr. Wood began mentally to list the inconveniences of doing business with a peer of the realm, Lord Sarre spoke.

"I admire your father and grandfather exceedingly, Mr. Wood. They have assured themselves an esteemed place in history with such a talent for design. And their promotion of a city built solely for health and leisure, like Bath, was a revolutionary idea. Now it is all the rage. If I were to put up the blunt for just such another holiday resort, I would wish to feel that it is unique in some way." He paused.

"Yes, my lord?" Mr. Wood prompted with eager deference.

"If you can indeed create some lodgings and assembly rooms in Bleadon exactly in accordance with the plan you showed me last week, I would consider myself committed to the project."

Mr. Wood's eyes shone with excitement. "I am prepared to convince you of it. How may I do so?"

"What I would like to do is meet you in Bleadon in a day or two. While there, we can visit each of the areas settled on for rooms to be built. I am a cautious man, Mr. Wood, and must see and understand as much as you do about this project. It is very important to me."

"I understand, my lord," responded the little businessman, not understanding in the least, but unwilling to interrogate a superior. There was a whole bonnet full of possibilities as to why a viscount with a reputedly large fortune and an estate in Gloucester would want to occupy himself in the design and promotion of a seaside resort. But to Mr. Wood, the most likely possibility was that the nobleman had gamed away his fortune and was up to his ears in debt. Probably with borrowed money and promissory notes, the viscount was looking to build a peaceful village into a bustling resort, drawing visitors who either hoped the salubrious air and bracing sea bathing would restore their health, or provide the prosperous middle class with something to do.

In the meantime, as chief proprietor, the viscount could begin to count his pence and pounds with an easier mind. As long as his lordship knew that *he* did not work without a considerable advance on the salary agreed upon, Mr. Wood did not care a fig as to why a nobleman had lowered himself to rub elbows with the working class.

"And Mr. Wood," the viscount continued, breaking into the gentleman's speculations and fixing him with a penetrating gaze. "Discretion is of the utmost importance. I do not wish anyone, outside of yourself and your most trusted assistants, to know that I am undertaking this project."

"My lord, you have nothing to fear from me! Assuming that you would wish to conduct your business affairs privately, I've not even mentioned your name to my personal assistant. He knows you only as the client who wishes to develop Bleadon. That is all."

Lord Sarre nodded approvingly. "I knew I would enjoy doing business with you, Mr. Wood. You are a credit to your lineage! I'll be in touch. I think the trip to Bleadon should be accomplished soon. Good day." He tipped his hat slightly, and removing his gold watch from a waistcoat pocket, observed the time. Closing the timepiece with a decided snap, he set out for the Pump Room at a good clip. First business, now pleasure. He smiled absently as he strode along, and a comely servant girl in a mob-cap who was passing by took the handsome viscount's pleasant expression as a personal compliment and skipped happily home to shuck peas and preen herself in the silver serving tray.

"DASH IT, GEORGE! That's the third time you've spilt that foul stuff on my coat! What's the matter with you?" Micah had removed his handkerchief from his pocket and was rubbing at the dark stain a splash of Bath mineral waters had made on the sleeve of his powder-blue jacket. His usual amiable expression was replaced by one of irritated displeasure.

"I beg your pardon, Micah! I can't think why I'm so clumsy this morning!" George replied sweetly, her large blue eyes wide and innocent. "But perhaps you'd best not stand quite so close to me as before!"

"Your mother asked me to escort you to fetch a cup, and I have. Now she is not to be seen and I will not abandon you to the crush of this dashed crowd!"

"Yes, it is a *very* large crowd, isn't it," George agreed, affecting the simpering air of a besotted schoolgirl.

Micah glared at her suspiciously. "I am beginning to suspect that you are purposely trying to make me miserable, George," growled her old playmate.

The foolish expression George had assumed to annoy her friend fell from her face. "Tit for tat, Micah!" she answered in a low, angry voice. "Your silly play-acting at dinner last night has certainly made *me* miserable! Now I am forced to come out a full month before I might have, and all because you have contrived some sort of stupid farradiddle about wishing to see me at the Upper Rooms and engaging me for the first set! I demand to know what nonsensical notion you've conceived in that skull of yours!"

Micah began to blink. Pulling out a silver fob from an inner waistcoat pocket, he appeared to be trying to ascertain the time through rapidly fluttering eyelids. Finally succeeding, he muttered, "Half past eleven," then replaced the watch and peered over the plumed headdresses and tall beaver hats of the crowd towards the narrow entrance doors of the Pump Room. Suddenly, his brow cleared and he heaved a small sigh.

George turned to see what had evidently removed Micah's pained expression and saw a tall, beaver-crowned gentleman working his way through the crowd towards them. There was something about the set of his shoulders and the fluid stride of his long, shapely legs encased in white unmentionables... Gradually his face came into focus.

"Why, it's you!"

"How do you do, Miss Georgiana Lacy?" said Tony with a smooth bow. "Morning, Micah!"

George smiled with unrestrained delight into the laughing green eyes of her new friend. While he smiled back at her, George seemed incapable of speaking. Then, recollecting herself, she exclaimed, "But Micah, why didn't you mention my meeting with your friend last night at dinner? Though I'm glad you did *not* in front of my mother, I've been wondrous curious...."

"Well, I... Mean to say, George, I didn't..." spluttered Micah.

"I asked Micah not to speak of it," interrupted Tony. "You had indicated that perhaps your mother wouldn't approve of your talking to a stranger, and I felt honour-bound to keep it our secret. But since Micah is an old playmate and a friend . . ."

"There are friends, and there are *friends,*" returned George with a quelling look at Micah. "Yet I believe he is still enough of a friend that he'll not tell my mother."

She glared at Micah until he jerked rather violently and blurted out, "Assure you, George! Dash it all! Can certainly count on me! The old . . . your mother won't get the skinny from me! M'lips are sealed!"

"Good!" George said with satisfaction and with an arch glance at her elegant new friend. "And now you must properly introduce the two of us."

"Shall I?" Micah looked at Tony.

"Proceed," Tony replied with a wary expression which puzzled George, but piqued her curiosity still further.

Just as Micah was about to perform the formalities, he suddenly drew himself up as stiff as a lamppost and gazed across the Pump Room with evident misgiving. Mrs. Lacy and Isabella had seen them and were approaching, inspiring as much admiration, awe and fear in their progress across the room as might be expected for two such tall, magnificent ladies. As the crowd stepped aside for the women to pass, George was forcefully reminded of the parting of the Red Sea.

She dreaded the necessity of introducing Tony to her mother and sister because she did not want her new friend to be put off by their arrogant manners. Since he was only an acquaintance of Micah's, she was sure they would not deem him worthy of their notice and would act accordingly.

"Lord Sarre," gushed Mrs. Lacy, tapping him lightly on the arm with her oriental-print fan. "How do you come to know Georgiana? I'm persuaded that someone must have told you she is Isabella's sister."

George couldn't believe her ears. Was Tony the Lord Somebody-or-other her mother and Isabella had been pursuing? But of course! Anthony, Lord Sarre *was* the name they'd spoken of so lovingly between them! How could she have failed to make a connection? Good gad, when she thought of all the things she'd said to him yesterday about Isabella and about her mother's avaricious plans to marry her sister off to a rich nobleman, she felt she ought to creep away to hide in a dark corner! He'd known all along that she was sharing information he oughtn't to hear! She had a sudden, overwhelming urge to box his lordship's aristocratic ears!

"Good morning, Miss Lacy, Mrs. Lacy," the viscount murmured over each grand lady's hand. "But I beg your pardon, I must advise you of your mistake. I did not know until just now that this young lady was another of your beautiful daughters, Mrs. Lacy."

What a bold-faced lie! thought George to herself. Yet *she* had kept her meeting with Tony a secret from her mother to avoid trouble. Wasn't that a form of lying, too? She frowned. It was too puzzling!

"It is Mr. Shelby who claims my acquaintance," the viscount continued. "I went to school with his older brother, Tom. I was delighted to discover that Micah had returned to the neighbourhood yesterday."

Micah smiled nervously and tipped his hat while Mrs. Lacy and Isabella stared at him with cool astonishment. Though their surprise was evident that Micah had friendly connections of some importance, the two ladies quickly absorbed the information and went on to the matters at hand.

"Isn't it a lovely day, Lord Sarre?" cooed Isabella, tossing the gleaming curls that lay gracefully against her neck.

"It is fair outside, my dear Miss Lacy, but fairer still *inside*," the viscount suavely responded, inclining his head in her direction.

George watched, appalled, as her new-found friend made a gudgeon of himself over her sister. She supposed this was accepted behaviour amongst the haute ton, but she had not expected Tony to participate so whole-heartedly. Could this tall, impeccably dressed gentleman, who so easily spewed forth a fulsome compliment to her sister, be the same man she'd sat by the stream with yesterday? He'd seemed so thoroughly sensible and likeable then. And even though he'd mistaken her for a servant at first, his apology had been genuine. Genuine—now that was how she'd have described the Tony she'd met by the stream; Lord Sarre, on the other hand, seemed to be someone quite different.

But then there was always the possibility that his lordship was truly smitten with her sister, and the compliments sincere. She could hardly credit the idea, though, since she'd candidly revealed to him many of her sister's faults in the course of their conversation yesterday. But then, George realized, she could not comprehend all the inner workings of a gentleman's mind and did not know whether the faults she had spoken of would be deemed faults by him at all.

While George's thoughts had gone wandering, the rest of them had been talking of the Bath waters; those for drink and those used to bathe in. Her attention was gained when one of the gouty old gentleman who frequented the Pump Room in the sincere pursuit of improved health, fell against Isabella when his crutch slipped on the polished floor. He really only brushed against her back and repositioned the hem of her skirt slightly, but Isabella was incensed.

"Ye gods, man! Cannot you be more careful?" she exclaimed, the vehemence of her emotions distorting her angelic countenance into something fearful. "You tumble my gown!" The poor man skulked away, muttering apologies. Her mother paid no heed to the occurrence, but George was always embarrassed for Isabella and for each and every victim of her frequent fits of ill temper, and felt herself blushing furiously. When she looked at the two gentlemen to observe their reaction she saw that Micah was thoroughly absorbed in tapping his cane against the bottom of his shoe, while the viscount's gaze was fixed on some point across the room, his face impassive and unreadable.

Suddenly Lord Sarre turned to Isabella and asked, "Do you like to sea bathe, Miss Lacy?"

George had heard her sister's opinion on sea bathing before. Isabella hated it. She'd tried it once and couldn't stand the stray grain or two of sand which had lodged between her toes, or the tiny shred of seaweed which had so inconsiderately floated by and sent her fastidious nerves into a flutter of revulsion. But before Isabella could voice an opinion, her mother spoke up, saying, "Do *you* like sea bathing, my lord?"

"I enjoy it excessively. There is nothing quite so refreshing as a bracing sea bath, I say."

Isabella had begun to turn up her nose, but wisely assumed a happy, compliant expression and said, "One never tires of the sea, does one? I love bathing above anything!" Then, rather encouraged by the viscount's approving smile and feeling quite sure that no sea bathing expedition was forthcoming, she added, "'Tis a pity that no one in our circle goes to the sea these days. Bristol is a shocking crush, quite overrun by hordes of commoners intent upon bathing in the sea just because they suppose it is fashionable. If only there were a nice, elegant little resort nearby..."

"Ah, but I have the perfect solution, my dear Miss Lacy," said Lord Sarre with a gleam in his eye. "I have an uncle, a widower, living in Bleadon, a nice, small village south of Bristol. His house is large and commodious and within yards of the sea. It is not precisely a resort, but there are one or two bathing machines in operation. My uncle has been wanting me to visit him for some time and I'd planned to leave Bath soon to do just that. Might I suggest that we make a party of it? All of us?'' He lifted an upturned palm and indicated the entire group with a sweeping gesture.

Nothing could have equalled Isabella's surprise, and George was hard-pressed not to break out in the giggles. She imagined the many conflicting emotions warring in her sister's bosom. On the one hand, Lord Sarre had announced that he planned to leave Bath soon in order to visit his uncle, perhaps too soon to allow Isabella's charms to have worked their full power on his sensibilities. On the other hand, if they accompanied him to Bleadon, she would have ample opportunity to practise her wiles. But she would have to bathe in the sea, which was, in her frequently expressed opinion, a huge, agitated puddle of dirty water inhabited by a preponderance of slimy plant life and odious sea creatures.

In the end, Isabella's affection for Lord Sarre's title, and several kicks on the ankle from her mother, settled the matter. "I should love to go to Bleadon," announced Isabella with forced delight.

"Yes," concurred Mrs. Lacy in trilling accents, her chest inflating with the import of his invitation. "Though Mr. Lacy cannot abide the sea, he will not wish to keep myself and Isabella from such a delightful excursion.''

"Micah?" the viscount looked at his friend, who, after a little hesitation, blurted out, "Er... pleased to go! Nothing better to do! That is...dashed pleased to go!"

"And Miss Georgiana Lacy will come, too?" Lord Sarre continued. "I insist that she join us. If Miss Isabella Lacy is the only young woman present she will be overcome by all our eager gallantries."

Though it was hardly likely that Isabella would be overcome by an excess of gallantries, George supposed that her mother had no recourse but to allow her younger daughter to be included in the party. And since Micah would be there too, it seemed the most expeditious way of getting both couples together for the purpose of courtship. Since Mrs. Lacy was, above all else, a practical woman, she overcame her reluctance to put up with George's oddities and graciously accepted his lordship's invitation for them all.

George's emotions were in a tumble! How could she remain angry at Tony when he'd purposely included her in such a delightful scheme? George had only been to the sea once, when she was eight years old. She remembered the frothing, blue swell of ocean with a child's mind. The salt smell of it, the brisk feel of it against her goose-bumped skin, the sandy beach stretching out below a congenial sun, the cool breezes that tangled her hair, and the gentle, surging waves that tugged at her ankles were all vivid in her memory.

So exhilarating were her thoughts that George felt it behooved her to hide them. She excused herself and retreated to where the maidservant was dispensing water to fetch another cup, which, like the other she'd procured, she had no intention of drinking. Since Mrs. Lacy was too engrossed in fawning over the viscount to bully Micah into joining her, and Micah was too fond of his blue coat to expose it to further abuse, George was able to get away with hardly any notice being taken of her.

Therefore her surprise was extreme when a moment or two later she lifted her sparkling, memory-glazed eyes to find Lord Sarre standing beside her.

"Oh!" she exclaimed, her hand jerking and sloshing the mineral waters onto the viscount's coat sleeve. "I beg your pardon!" George cried earnestly. "I assure you I didn't *mean* to do it! Really I did not!"

Lord Sarre raised amused brows and said, "Don't fret, poppet. Why should I think you did it expressly? You're not such a mischief-maker as that, are you? Besides, it's of no consequence." He looked at the stain of water on his coat, flicked a negligent finger over it and shrugged.

George was torn between feelings of gratitude that the viscount was not such a fuss-budget about his clothes as other young men she could mention, and guilt over her very real attempts at mischief earlier when she'd thoroughly baptized Micah's blue coat. Then she remembered that what she ought to be feeling was anger! She nursed her anger now, hoping to fan it into full heat again. After all, Lord Sarre had purposely withheld his identity when they'd met by the stream and had allowed her to express opinions and feelings that were best left unexpressed, given the fact that he knew the parties much better than he'd led her to suppose.

"Now, George, don't curl your lip at me like that,' admonished the viscount. "I thought we were friends!"

"A friend would not allow a person to make a complete cake of herself. You should have told me who you were! It was very wrong of you!"

The maidservant holding the crystal pitcher looked expectantly at the viscount and he requested two cups of water. While she was filling them, he leaned closer to George and said, "Do you really think anything you said to me was a revelation? Do you honestly believe me so stupid as to be entirely in the dark about your sister's ambitions regarding me? And lastly, do you imagine that anything you said changed my intentions one whit? The answer, my little poppet, to all these questions is 'no.'"

George was stunned by Lord Sarre's words. She stood with a blank look on her face for some time before the steady influence of a pair of intense green eyes nudged her back into consciousness. "Do you mean to say, sir," she enquired wonderingly, "that nothing I said shocked you, and that you think of Isabella in just such a light as you did before?"

"Indeed I do. My opinion of Isabella has not changed one jot," he responded matter-of-factly. "Now, to get on to something I find to be a deal more interesting, do *you* like to sea bathe, Miss Georgiana Lacy?"

George's eyes sparkled again at the very thought of the sea. "I don't know, precisely! I've only waded a bit before. But I think I should like sea bathing very much . . . very much indeed!"

"Just as I supposed," said the viscount, a wide, warm smile. of satisfaction spreading over his handsome features.

THE ASSEMBLY at the Upper Rooms had to be given up so the ladies might prepare for the journey to Bleadon, which Lord Sarre had decided to undertake the following morning, sending word ahead to his uncle of their imminent arrival. This left Micah no alternative but to express his extreme unhappiness in being denied a set of dances with George. When no one was looking, George expressed *her* feelings about the loss of a set of country dances with Micah by sticking out her tongue. After affecting the proper degree of affront at her behaviour, he let out a shout of laughter which drew all eyes in the Pump Room to their little group. Considerably cowed by the glower he encountered in both Mrs. Lacy's and Isabella's eyes, Micah endeavoured to avoid looking at George altogether. In this way he hoped to preserve the peace.

Morning came, following such a night of packing and lamentations as George had never experienced before. Isabella complained that Bleadon was an inconsequential little town with no fashion, no people worth knowing and no millinery shops worth patronizing. And she abhorred sea bathing! If not for the viscount's title and fortune, she would as lief stay home.

George listened with half an ear, personally thrilled to be taking a trip to a part of the country she longed to see. And Lord Sarre—Tony—would be there. Even if he did show a singular lack of taste in his admiration of Isabella, George had decided to grant him the possession of this one fault, her anger on all points quite extinguished. She supposed that admiration of beauty without substance was a weakness indulged in by most of the male sex. He could still be her friend, after all.

Mr. Lacy was a little bewildered by the sudden decision to post off to Bleadon in such a hurry. He remembered it only as a little seaside town in which his horse had once thrown a shoe, and it was the devil of a time he'd had finding a smithy to assist him. But ladies would have their whims, he supposed. And Mrs. Lacy had informed him that the host of the house in which they'd reside for the proposed two weeks would be unexceptionable. Admiral Braithwaite was, after all, uncle of Lord Sarre. There could be no greater recommendation.

It was decided that the trip could be accomplished with just two carriages, and since the Viscount did not travel by himself in a coach and four, Micah and Mr. Lacy supplied the transportation.

Such clatter, such crunching of gravel and snorts of impatience from the prancing horses! George loved the sound and bustle of departure! She leaned out of her bedchamber window and looked down on the front courtyard. She was dressed in a simple white muslin, which she had chosen because it would be cool and comfortable to travel in. Her half-boots and bonnet were a plain beige colour and very practical. Unlike Isabella, she did not have shoes and hats to match every gown. But the hat was trimmed with one jaunty blue feather Perkins had gleaned from Isabella's bounteous supply of frills and furbelows, and it managed to become her despite her complete lack of interest in appearing attractive.

For someone who had so recently preferred the company of her books and her dog to people, George felt positively festive. There was Whiskers now, happily cantering about the yard, determined to be a part of the hubbub by getting in the way.

Whiskers! How could the welfare of her pet have so entirely escaped her? What to do about Whiskers? None of the servants could be depended upon to feed the poor thing properly, and he was so disobedient they would soon have him locked in the cellar, perhaps forgetting him altogether! And since her father frequently forgot to feed even himself, he definitely could not be applied to, to keep her pet from the appalling possibility of starvation!

"George. *Georgiana!* What are you about, gel? Come down this instant! His lordship and Micah are arrived," came her mother's strident voice from below.

George descended the stairs in deep thought, but every possible solution to the dilemma her mind conceived eventually met with an insurmountable obstacle. As she walked outside into the sunlit morning, Whiskers ran up to her and placed his dusty paws on her knees.

"George! You'll dirty your gown, child! Push that scruffy dog down, I say!" called her mother from the carriage in which she was already comfortably ensconced.

"But Mama," said George, with feeling, "what am I to do about Whiskers? What if the servants do not feed him? What if they do not let him in when there is a thunderstorm? You know how very frightened he is of the thunder and lightning!"

"Oh, for heaven's sake, George! Can't you see that Lord Sarre wishes to be off? We can't dally about here while you wax sentimental over a silly dog! Come, get into the carriage!"

George began to feel foolish. She knew that she was being observed by several pair of eyes. There stood Lord Sarre at his horse's head, prepared to mount, but his face was turned away. Micah was already mounted, the horse prancing impatiently and absorbing his attention entirely. But Isabella and her mother glared at her from one carriage, while the two abigails and two valets stared fixedly at her from the other. From no one did she perceive a softening of features or a sympathetic smile, until the viscount turned round. Handing his horse's lead to a footman, Lord Sarre walked across the short space of gravel to stand before her. Though he did not absolutely smile, the expression on his face gave her reason to hope.

"Miss Lacy, no solution to this problem presents itself to me at the moment...."

Her head and her hopes sank together.

"Unless..."

Her head and her hopes lifted in unison.

"Unless we take the hairy little beast with us!"

Then, to the amazement of all, Lord Sarre lifted the dog in his arms and carried him to the carriage in which Mrs. Lacy and Isabella were seated. Placing the dog in dignified state against the squabs directly opposite the two stupefied ladies and handing George up into the carriage after her pet, he then closed the door.

It was some moments after the carriage had begun its bumpy progress over rutted roads that any of the ladies found the presence of mind to speak, and then it was Isabella who broke the silence. Looking over at her sister, whose mirth-filled eyes bespoke a definite lack of refinement, and at an unkempt dog lolling his scraggly head and drooling tongue out of the window, Miss Isabella Marguerite Lacy could only say, in the tone of one wholly overcome by revulsion, "Ye gods!"

CHAPTER FOUR

THE TRIP WAS ACCOMPLISHED without any major mishap and only delayed by perhaps an hour by Whiskers, whose frequent noisy demands to be let out of the coach were, out of cautiousness, never denied. Once, while investigating some gorse bushes on a particularly uninviting stretch of health, he wandered away. Lord Sarre, Micah and George were compelled to search the area for some fifteen minutes before he chose to reveal himself. Proudly holding a fat field mouse in his sharp little teeth, he stood on his hind legs at the opened coach door, where an irritated Isabella and Mrs. Lacy sat, vigorously fanning themselves and swatting flies.

To their credit, neither lady swooned, but neither would they endure that the "horrid little beast" be allowed back inside the hallowed confines of the coach. Whiskers finished the journey sitting up front with Freddy, the coachman, very well pleased with himself and only a little disappointed that he was forced to leave behind the spoils of his hunt.

For Lord Sarre the journey was much less satisfying. Micah had been Friday-faced and tight-lipped all morning, and just as they reached the outskirts of

Bleadon the viscount determined to come to the bottom of it.

"We shall have little private conversation the rest of the day, Micah, so I suggest you empty your budget now, my friend," he began in a coaxing manner. "I know something has you blue-deviled and I wish you would come out with it."

"Dash it, Tony," exclaimed Micah. "One thing I'd like t'know! Do you know what you're doing? Throwing out lures to a chit's sister ain't my notion of courting a girl! If you keep dangling your title like a carrot in front of Isabella's nose and encouraging her with those idiotic odes to her beauty, you may find yourself leg-shackled to the wrong girl!"

"Calm yourself, Micah," responded the viscount soothingly. "I haven't decided that I want to be leg-shackled to anyone just yet. George is a taking little thing, to be sure . . ." He looked back at the carriage and saw her golden head sticking out of the window. She was waving at Whiskers. He smiled despite himself. "But who's to say I won't find her a dead bore in a matter of days," he added philosophically. But when he looked at Micah for confirmation, that gentleman's dubious look proved his argument unconvincing. "Such has always been the case before!" Lord Sarre insisted.

"Never seen you go to such trouble over any woman, Tony! Not even that ripe 'un from Covent Garden. And George don't even want to bring you up to scratch! Only wants to be your friend! Using her sister as an excuse to be near her ain't the thing to do! Going to find yourself in a devilish mess, I say!"

"Never fear that I'll put myself in a compromising position where Isabella is concerned," said the viscount, a look of distaste passing over his features at the mere thought of it. "A casual flirtation does not require consummation in the exchanging of vows."

"I still say watch yourself, Tony! Mrs. Lacy has a devious mind!"

"I'll be careful, Micah. Don't worry," his lordship reassured his friend, assuming a bored voice so that the topic would be dropped. He almost wished he hadn't encouraged Micah to speak his mind. It was disconcerting to be warned against a misalliance with Isabella, when the real danger lay in his attraction to George. It wasn't likely he'd be bored with that faerie-bred creature in a lifetime, and that thought frightened him more than he wished to admit to Micah or anyone, and least of all to himself.

REGARDLESS OF THE DUST kicked up by the horses, George could not resist sneaking the window down for another peek out of the carriage without the hindrance of the dirtied glass to obscure her view. While Isabella and her mother napped, George saw Bleadon for the first time without an ongoing critical commentary.

It was a pleasant little town, crammed full of tidy cottages with heavy stone walls and sturdy shutters. Built to serve as a kind of fortress against the sea, they were wedged so closely together they seemed practically on top of one another, and the gardens were so small they were no more than patches of grass with a few primroses. The roads that wound between them were exceedingly narrow, and though George could appreciate the picturesque in all she saw, the whole effect was rather close. Where was the sea? she wondered. If not for the distinct salt smell of it wafting on the breeze, one might never know the beach was only a brisk walk away from this battened-down little village.

At last the cottages thinned out. As they began to ascend a hill, the road broadened considerably. The houses they passed now stood much more to themselves, were of a modern design and were constructed of a lovely white stone. After straining upwards for a few minutes, the horses were finally guided off the main road and through private lodge gates belonging to a house of substantial size.

As they entered the courtyard, George craned her neck out of the carriage window to gaze up at the building and was a little frightened to discover a very tall man standing on the flagged steps to receive them in state. Never had she seen anyone with such a straight back and upright posture. His hair was a startling silver-white, and his eyebrows and mustache were so bushy they seemed nearly to hide his eyes and mouth. And even more interesting was the fact that the gentleman (whom George assumed was Admiral Braithwaite) was not alone. A young woman stood at his side. She was as tall as Isabella, but certainly not as voluptuous.

"By God, Tony, it's damned good to see you," shouted the admiral, crushing the viscount to his barrel-like chest and thumping him soundly on the back.

When Tony could catch his wind, he answered, "Uncle Jacob, always a pleasure! And Jane! I didn't expect to see you here. Thought you were touring the Lake District with Aunt Phoebe and Uncle Ned."

"I left them at Crooklands and posted home," Jane answered in a soft, cultured voice and with a deep-dimpled smile. "I must have somehow known you were coming." She extended a hand and Tony kissed it, returning her smile quite genuinely.

During this little tête-à-tête, Micah had been handing the ladies out of the carriage, but all that transpired had been seen. As a result, Isabella had already taken a strong dislike to Jane. Unwilling to share her quarry's notice with anyone, Isabella's eyes sparkled with malice. But prepared to do the pretty for appearances' sake, she smiled quite convincingly throughout the introductions.

When the admiral was introduced to George, she was delighted to discover his eyes to be the same lustrous colour as his nephew's and just as full of laughter and goodwill. George liked him immediately. She could not help but smile back at a pair of green eyes that were so exactly like Tony's, now could she? Jane's eyes were a softer hazel, and with her golden brown hair swept away from her face into a simple knot of wispy curls, she exuded a kind of serene elegance that Isabella's more blatant attractions had never attained.

"What a little shag-rag!" exclaimed Jane when Whiskers had jumped down from the coach to investigate his new surroundings. "What do you call it?"

"His name is Whiskers," replied George, her eyes anxiously watching Jane for some sign of disapproval. "He's mine. I must warn you, he'll undoubtedly try to follow me into the house. Have you a dislike of dogs, Miss Braithwaite?"

"Good heavens, no!" that lady expostulated with a laugh. "I used to have three myself! But I'm gone so frequently from home now that I gave them away to my nephews so they would not be lonely! And, please call me Jane. We needn't be so formal!"

"Only if you will call me George," George promptly responded, with a smile. How nice to have found a kindred spirit in Miss Braithwaite!

As it happened, the housekeeper was so busy taking care of Mrs. Lacy's and Isabella's immediate demands, it was Jane who showed George to her room. As they entered the large chamber, George was struck by the airiness of it. Daisied wallpaper covered the high walls, a yellow counterpane on the bed and light, delicately carved furniture lent the room a fresh, springlike air. French doors opened onto a balcony at one end, and in her excitement to discover the view they would allow, she threw her bonnet on the bed and hastened over to unlatch them.

"Oh, how delightful! How lucky you are to live here!" exclaimed George in her usual spontaneous manner when she had stepped onto the balcony. The back of the house faced the sea. Perhaps one hundred yards of green terraced lawn led to a sudden, steep cliff that plunged to a wide stretch of beach. And then there was the sea itself, in all its vastness, swelling and breaking against the shore.

"It will soon be high tide," commented Jane, moving to stand beside her and resting her hands on the balcony rail. "Just over there are the two bathing machines used by the ladies." She pointed up the beach and George observed what appeared to be tiny houses on wagons with huge wheels. "And quite in the opposite direction is the gentlemen's machine."

"Why is there only one for the men?" asked George. "Do fewer of them bathe?"

"No, I believe more men bathe than women," she replied with an impish smile. "Only most of the gentlemen dispense with the proprieties and find a secluded stretch of beach where they may swim without the benefit of a bathing machine, or...dare I say it...without bathing robes!"

George giggled. It appeared that Jane was quite as outspoken as herself!

"Do you mean to bathe, George?" she asked her now.

"Oh yes! I can't wait!" George answered eagerly.

"Well, then we shall go tomorrow!" said Jane, laughing delightedly at George's enthusiasm. "In the meantime I suggest that you freshen up and rest before dinner. Where's your abigail?''

"I share Perkins with Isabella. I don't require much fuss, you know," George advised the young woman. "But must I rest? I've been cooped up in the carriage all day and would like nothing better than a walk on the beach. Would you join me? Perhaps you could tell me all about this place, how you came to live here and all. I've a wondrous large curiosity."

"I've no doubt you do," responded Jane, her hazel eyes twinkling. Then, evidently seeing some movement below, she turned her head towards the lawn. "Why, it's Tony! Hallo!" She shouted at him and waved.

Lord Sarre had been standing with his hands on his hips at the very edge of the lawn, looking out at the sea. He'd removed his beaver hat, jacket and neckcloth and the wind rippled through his thick, dark hair. Lifting his hand to shade his eyes, he shouted back, "Hallo! Beautiful day!"

"So we've observed. Don't move, Tony!" Then, grabbing George by the hand, Jane swept them out of the room and down a back stairway, past the kitchen and into the yard. "We're going for a walk," Jane breathlessly informed the viscount when he stepped forward to meet them sporting a large smile. "And you may escort us, if you please!"

Lord Sarre inclined his head, raised an amused brow, and answered, "Well, if you do not mind my deshabille I would be delighted to escort you." Jane pooh-poohed his reservations about the informal arrangement of his clothes and soon they were following him down a narrow, gradually descending path which hugged the sides of the cliff. Frequently, if the path grew rather steep, he would turn and take their hands, guiding their footsteps until they had reached more level ground. Occasionally Jane would reach forward and place her open palm on his back, steadying herself or striving for support as she slid on a smooth stone.

It was odd, thought George, how solid and comforting the viscount's back appeared to her. And the way he looked round to watch their progress and help them seemed very kind, especially when he smiled so warmly. But she'd never dare to touch him, as Jane did. They'd only known each other three days, after all, while he and Jane were cousins and appeared very close and friendly with each other. Still, it made her feel a trifle envious each time Jane used that lovely back for a prop when she herself had only the rough walls of the cliff to rely on. And Whiskers certainly was no help, the way he scampered continually between her feet!

When they reached the beach, Lord Sarre moved between them and offered each an arm. George breathed a blissful sigh and turned to look at Jane. "Now you must tell me everything!"

"Everything?" the viscount's eyebrows shot up. "Then I would certainly be in your way. Sharing confidences is something you ladies generally do in private, isn't it?''

"Don't be stupid, Tony," Jane chided him with an affectionate smile. "George only wants to know about Neptune House and how we came to live here."

"Neptune House! What an odd name!" exclaimed George.

"It could have been Unicorn House, which is worse still," said Lord Sarre, laughing. "My uncle, as you must know, is retired from the Navy, but though he may have left the Navy, the Navy has never left him! The *Neptune* was one of the ships he commanded, a great man-of-war which fought valiantly for England at Trafalgar."

"Mother was partial to the *Unicorn,*" Jane continued, "because she lived on that ship with Father for several years. Then, when my older brother, Joseph, was born she decided to live in Bleadon. She did not fancy the idea of having a sick child and the physician several days' voyage away! Joseph never forgave her for the decision, I believe! He's in the Navy now, too, and quite as addicted to the sea as my father. When Father retired, he built this house. Mother wanted to keep our snug cottage in the weald, well away from the full brunt of the winds and weather one gets living on the coast. But Father insisted that he wanted to build his house on a hill with a view of the sea."

"I'm in complete agreement with your father," said George with conviction.

"You might not agree if there happens to be one of our famous storms during your visit here!" suggested Jane.

"And Whiskers doesn't like thunder and lightning," the viscount reminded George with a wink.

"But he certainly does like dirtying my gowns!" she said, disengaging her arm from Lord Sarre's and brushing off the sandy paw-prints Whiskers had just left on her skirt. "He wants to play, I suppose. I'd best find a stick and help him run off his fidgets, or else I won't settle him down at all tonight!"

With that George began to search for a piece of driftwood small enough to suit her purpose. She'd progressed a few yards down the beach away from the others before she found a suitable stick and began to toss it into the very shallow waves at the edge of the surf for Whiskers to retrieve. Whiskers made a game of trying to beat the tide for possession of the stick, and waded in deep enough to immerse his stubby legs to the halfway mark. He was doing quite well at snatching the stick from the frothy fingers of the surf until a rather large wave came along unexpectedly and sucked the piece of wood farther out where the tide was deeper. There it stuck upright in the wet sand.

When it appeared that Whiskers meant to go after the stick regardless of the waves, which would certainly break over the top of him, George decided that a rescue was in order. She glanced back towards Jane and Tony and discovered them in earnest conversation, so earnest, in fact, that they appeared oblivious of their surroundings. Taking advantage of their preoccupation, she quickly pulled off her shoes and stockings and tossed them on the sand. She picked up her skirts and waded into the shallow water to save her pet from drowning, or at the very least, from the cold shock of an unexpected sea bath.

She shooed Whiskers back onto the beach and adjured him to sit. Then she waded back in and dislodged the stick, throwing it up onto the shore where her pet might safely chase it. Now she supposed she ought to return as well, but was so enjoying the refreshing sensation of cool water up to her knees that she was disinclined to move. She stood there for some time, relishing the cool sea air against her cheek, the sun glancing off the water and the drifts of flowing sand beneath her feet that tickled her soles so deliciously.

Still Tony and Jane talked. The viscount had looked over at her, smiling, when she'd first waded into the sea, but he'd turned back to Jane almost immediately. George was suddenly struck with the seriousness of their expressions. Far enough away that she could not hear what they said, but still close enough that she might observe their faces, she saw Tony take hold of Jane's hands and look at her rather tenderly. As he spoke to her, with a most earnest countenance, Jane blushed and dropped her head.

Good gad, was it possible that the viscount, that Tony, was in love with his cousin? George was caught quite off guard by the emotions such a possibility produced in her. Though she had been disgusted by his apparent admiration of Isabella, she had accepted it as inevitable. Gentleman were always attracted to Isabella; they couldn't seem to help themselves. But if Tony were attracted to his cousin, Jane, it was undoubtedly based on a stronger foundation than the mere possession of good looks. He'd known Jane his entire life. And George instinctively knew, even after such a short acquaintance, that Jane had qualities any sensible, right-hearted man would esteem.

How differently George felt about an attachment between Tony and Jane, rather than between Tony and Isabella! Isabella would only be a wife (and not a very good one at that!) but Jane would be a wife *and* a friend....

"George! Look out!"

Jolted out of her disturbing reverie by Lord Sarre's warning, George looked up to see that both he and Jane wore expressions of extreme dismay. Before she could discover the source of their agitation, George was pushed off her feet by a wall of boiling sea water, carried with unceremonious speed to the shore, and dumped face down in a tangled heap of soaked muslin at his lordship's feet.

Quite unharmed but thoroughly humiliated, George was scooped up by the viscount and carried to dry land.

"Better fetch a blanket, Jane. Do it quickly," George heard him order in a low, contained voice.

"Do not disturb the servants for assistance, if you understand my meaning."

"Of course," was Jane's reply as she hurried away.

Pushing the drenched locks of hair out of her eyes, George was about to protest that she wasn't the least bit cold and could certainly manage the walk back to the house without a blanket, when she discovered a very real need for one. Her dip in the sea had rendered her thin muslin gown and the gauzy chemise underneath transparent. Unable to utter anything remotely sensible under the circumstances, George could only moan "Oh, no!" in the most mortified of accents and drew her knees up to her chest, wrapping her arms around them and hiding her burning face in her hands.

The viscount still knelt beside her, his arm in a protective gesture about her shoulders. Whiskers hovered nearby, alternately whimpering and sitting up on his hind legs. Occasionally George would moan and shake her head, her face still hidden in her hands.

"If I had a coat, I should lend it to you," said the viscount in a very kind voice, serving only to make George feel all the more wretched. "You must be cold."

"I'm not cold at all," replied George petulantly, her voice muffled. "And you know it! What I am, to be exact, is very improperly unclothed and in the company of a member of the opposite sex! You needn't beat about the bush, trying to be polite. I may be clumsy, but I'm not blind!'' She paused, then muttered, "Though, at this moment, I wish *you* were!"

"So do I, poppet," answered the viscount, and George thought she detected a wry edge of amusement in his voice. She could not help it, she must raise her own eyes to observe his. If he were amused, the emotion would surely be reflected there. And if he thought her foolish and pitied her, or stupid and clumsy and was repulsed by her, any of these feelings might be obvious from the expression on his face. She steeled herself for the worst and lifted her eyes.

If someone had asked George what the viscount was feeling, which she was so sure she'd be able to discover by looking into his eyes, she'd have been nonplussed. No one had ever looked at her in just that way before! He was flushed, his whole countenance and expression seeming to glow with an inner fire. His eyes were softly illuminated, yet intensely penetrating. His mouth curved in a slight smile, but there was restraint and tension in each feature of his face.

The whole effect was alarming to George, but in a way she did not understand. A shudder rippled down her spine and nestled in a warm pool somewhere in the region of her stomach. It was a frightening sensation, but very pleasant. And the whole idea of something being frightening and pleasant at the same time did not make one jot of sense to her.

"Why didn't *you* fetch the blanket, Tony?" George blurted out, in an effort to break the spell his strange look was weaving over her senses. "It might have spared us both some embarrassing moments if you had done so!''

As if it were an effort to speak while he looked at her, the viscount cleared his throat and turned his face towards the sea. ''Jane knows where the linen closet is. I don't. And I don't want anyone to know that I was with you when this happened. If I had gone up to the house and demanded a blanket, then everyone would know I had been present and seen you . . . like this.''

''Ah, yes. Because it would embarrass me to know that *they* all knew! How very thoughtful you are, Tony!'' Disregarding her misery, George attempted to smile.

Lord Sarre turned to look at her again. ''No, George,'' he explained slowly and seriously. ''It is because your mother would insist that I marry you. You may not realize this, my dear girl, but though it is only an accident, this situation could be easily perceived as compromising to your honour! Especially if one wishes to see it in such a light!''

George's mouth fell open in shock and alarm. She would never want anyone to be forced to marry her against his will, especially Tony! And especially since he appeared to be in love with his cousin. ''Oh, no, Tony! No, it can't be like that! I won't . . . I can't . . .'' George was so upset she allowed her legs to straighten and she grabbed his forearm with her two hands, the knuckles whitening with the strength of her grip.

Could she have imagined it, she wondered, or did she detect a flicker of something like hurt flit across Tony's features? Then when his eyes seemed to drop involuntarily to her wet dress and quickly jerk back to her face, she realized that she'd forgotten her shameful state. Quickly, she pulled her knees up against her chest again and released her grip on his arm.

"That is precisely why I mean to keep my part of this episode a secret, George. Marriage should only be entered into by two *willing* partners." He smiled then, though it was only a weak endeavour, not at all deserving to be compared with his usual smile. Then a wave of relief washed over his features and he sighed. "Here is Jane at last."

"Uncle Jacob, may I say this is the best ragout I've ever tasted!" said Lord Sarre, his eyes determinedly turned to the admiral at his left to avoid looking across the table at George.

"You may say it if you wish, Tony," replied the admiral in his gruff baritone. "But I'm damned it I know what you mean. That's a fricasseed chicken if I ever saw one. Not a damned vegetable in the dish!"

"So I see," said the viscount, soberly inspecting the contents of his plate.

"It's that widgeon of a French cook he's got at Aldsworth, Admiral," offered Micah, by way of an apology for his friend's culinary faux pas. "Has Tony's mind all mucked up with too much Béarnaise sauce. Ha!"

"French cook or no, Tony, you're a thousand miles away tonight," observed the admiral, glaring at his nephew from under the shade of his protruding eyebrows.

"Well, I . . ." began the viscount.

"Perhaps it was that long nap you took when we arrived this afternoon, Lord Sarre, which is making you feel not quite the thing," advised Mrs. Lacy, who was sitting on the other side of the admiral, resplendent in rubies and a scarlet marmeluke cap. "Didn't you say you'd fallen asleep directly and only awakened in time for dinner? Sometimes when I sleep too long I get the worst megrim, you can't imagine! The best thing for it is just a dash of laudanum in a small tumbler of claret. Always works for me, doesn't it, Isabella?"

"And thank the Lord it does," drawled Isabella disrespectfully, ignoring her mother's responding look of irritation. Sitting to the right of Lord Sarre, Isabella was a vision of majesty in a gown of peacock blue with a pearlseeded bodice adding interest to the already substantial allure of her ample bosom. "But as for naps disagreeing with one, it is almost always the opposite case, isn't it? As for me, nothing refreshes or beautifies quite so much as a short nap of three or four hours. Perhaps Lord Sarre's health has been disordered by the sea air," she suggested, attempting to evince concern by languidly raising her arched brows.

"I'm overwhelmed by these gratifying expressions of concern for my health," the viscount responded acidly, and to no one in particular. "But mistaking a fricassee for a ragout hardly merits this much solicitude!"

"Dash it, Tony," said Micah, while they all stared at the viscount and wondered at the unusual discomposure of his nerves. "No need to bite off our noses!"

"Tony is only a little fatigued," broke in Jane, who had been anxiously observing the proceedings from the other end of the table. "What do you say we play a rubber of piquet after dinner, Tony? Or get up a Loo table? Beating me soundly at cards always dissipates Lord Sarre's fatigue!" she announced to the others with a trill of laughter only the most astute would have recognized as false.

Throwing off his ill humour with an effort, the viscount responded to his cousin's calculated sally with a weary, but appreciative smile. "Thank you, Jane," he said, his eyes conveying a deeper meaning. "Piquet it is."

He then proceeded to convince the rest of the party that his absence of mind and shortness of temper were a thing of the past. With the suave delivery they'd all come to expect of him, he recounted an amusing on-dit about Sally Jersey, the head patroness of the elite rooms at Almack's, and a young dandy who'd had the audacity to arrive at that reverenced hall of Society quite thoroughly foxed. At the end of the anecdote everyone was laughing. Everyone, that is, but George.

She had been the source of his preoccupation earlier, and the continued source of his concern now. When she'd timidly entered the drawing-room, just before dinner was announced, it was obvious she'd received a severe dressing-down from her mother for having been ruthlessly tackled by a wave of sea water. The viscount had found out from Jane that though she had explained to Mrs. Lacy that an occasional large wave unexpectedly appears when high tide is coming on, Mrs. Lacy insisted that George shouldn't have been in the water in the first place. And that she was trying to assist Whiskers in a game of fetch made it all the worse!

But the flush of colour which so persistently lingered on George's delicately rounded cheeks had to be more than just the result of her mother's scolding. Surely George was used to those. Nor could the telltale colour be left over from the hot bath she'd undoubtedly taken after her cool dip in the sea. He'd noticed the silken sheen of her freshly washed hair, still a little damp around the hairline, frizzing and curling in delicate, endearing wisps about her face.

Damn, why wouldn't she look at him? Of course she was embarrassed, but he'd tried desperately to put her at her ease when they'd first sat down to dinner. But when she'd seemed to shrink farther away whenever he addressed her, he finally determined not to look at her at all, if that was what she wanted. Thus he had ended up making that inane comment about the ragout—or rather the fricassee!

Thank God she couldn't read his mind, for then she'd surely die of shame! Ever since he'd pulled her out of the sea, whenever he looked at her he saw that elfin mop of hair plastered in glistening curls against her face and flopping into her eyes, her eyelashes laced with sand, and those small, pink-tipped breasts pressing against wet muslin.... He'd seen naked women before, of course, probably more than any man had a right to. But it wasn't just the supple beauty of her young body which made his loins burn with desire. It was simply because the body he'd seen belonged to George—George, the most original, fresh little baggage he'd ever come across in the whole of his dissipated twenty-eight years.

But to temper these warm thoughts came the sinking realization that she couldn't possibly have the same intensity of feelings for him. How could he ever forget the horrified look that had appeared on her face when he'd mentioned the possibility of a marriage between them?

"I say, Tony, shall we go sea bathing tomorrow?" Micah asked, breaking in on these decidedly unsuitable dinnertime thoughts. "The ladies are going. George and Jane and Isa—Miss Lacy, that is! Heard George took a plunge already today! Still want to go tomorrow, George?" Micah heckled his old playmate, elbowing her rather mercilessly beneath the cover of the hanging tablecloth.

Observing the first real sign of George's old spirit flaring up, Lord Sarre watched her blue eyes lift from the mound of peas she'd been squashing and pushing about with her fork and narrow warningly at Micah. "I shall not let one little wave spoil my enjoyment of the sea," she retorted, with a dignified lift of her pointed chin. Then, before she returned to the task of further mutilating her peas, she glanced briefly at the viscount. The expression in her eyes was unfathomable. He sighed, sincerely hoping that one little wave had not completely spoiled his chances, either.

CHAPTER FIVE

GEORGE SLIPPED OUT of the house and bent her steps towards the gates leading to the main road. It was still very early and the dew shimmered in crystal drops on the closely scythed grass and hung glistening on the neat rows of juniper which bordered the lawn. She had a brief thought that her half boots of cambric might not hold up against the dampness, but dismissed the concern almost immediately under the influence of such a glorious summer's morning. She had dressed in a simple pink-and-white sprigged gown of French muslin with a Norwich shawl draped around her shoulders to guard against a nip of coolness in the air. A white poke bonnet with a spray of pink roses at the crown framed her small face and sheltered her freckled nose from the sun.

Standing just outside the gates, she was looking first up the hill and then down, trying to decide which way to go when she heard Jane's voice from behind her.

"George! Stay a moment!"

George turned round and waited obediently, though she wasn't sure she wanted company and hoped Jane did not intend to accompany her. When Jane finally caught up with her, running across the lawn with bonnet in hand in order to do so, she looked so pleased and smiled so happily, George began to feel guilty for having begrudged the interruption. She smiled back and said, "I did not think anyone else would be up this early. I meant to have a walk before breakfast."

"Father is up at the cock's crow, or should I say the seagull's caw?" answered Jane breathlessly. She paused for a moment to tie the lavender bow of her bonnet securely beneath her chin. She looked as fresh and delicate as an Easter lily in her white crepe gown trimmed with embroidered violets, and George could not help but admire her. "I'm used to getting up with him so that we may have breakfast together," she continued. "Ever since Mother died, I've tried to do so. I cannot take her place, of course, but I like to think he misses her less if someone is across the table from him eating kippers as she used to do. But I've been gone so frequently during the last year, I believe he's sometimes lonely."

"Where have you been?" asked George, unable to curtail her curiosity even if it meant she might lose her opportunity for a private ramble.

"Well, if I may join you on your walk, I'll tell you," replied Jane, a question in her eyes as she smiled kindly at George. "I had a feeling you wanted to be alone this morning...." She paused, but George, kicking her toe against a rock in the road, did not respond. "But you were so quiet and withdrawn at dinner last night, I've been worried about you. I thought, instead of being alone, it might be better if you talked to someone." She took George's arm and tucked it snugly inside her own and steered her round to start walking up the hill together. "Let's go this way. I'll show you the mall of the place. It's quite a pretty view from up there."

George felt herself blushing from the perceptiveness of Jane's remarks and at the same time yielding to the ready sympathy she offered. She felt so foolish! Of course she was embarrassed about her mishap at the beach, but that wasn't all that was disturbing her. She hadn't quite puzzled it out yet, but she thought she might be jealous of Jane. Not in the same way that Isabella was jealous, of course, since George did not want to bring the viscount up to scratch, as the expression went. But she envied the closeness Jane seemed to share with him. It was reasonable that Tony should be on more intimate terms with his cousin than he was with her; after all, they'd only known each other a few days. But reason didn't seem to have anything to do with the way she felt.

"You know, George," Jane began, "if I were to be given a choice of any young man in the world whose company I might mortify myself in, it would probably be Tony."

"But he is your cousin, Jane," objected George. "Of course you would feel less embarrassment in such a case."

"Even if he were not my cousin!" Jane insisted with a decided nod of her head.

"Why do you say that?" asked George.

"Because no one is kinder or more understanding than Tony. He knows you are embarrassed, George, and it is causing him a good deal of distress to know he's the reason for it. He wishes more than anything to put you at your ease."

"Yes, I know. And I haven't been very cooperative," she admitted, sighing softly. "I suppose it cannot be undone, so I ought to make the best of it. It's either that or make both Tony and myself miserable."

"There!" cried Jane approvingly. "You're such a sensible girl, George. I knew you would come to my way of thinking! Now, to put the principle into practice, we will drop the subject altogether and never speak of it again, just as if it didn't happen! And you may trust Tony never to remind you!"

Already George had begun to feel better. Of course Jane was right. What was the use of fretting over spilled milk, or in this case, soaked muslin! And as for the other, her jealousy of Jane, she must try to repress it. Jane was a wonderful person, and if Tony wanted to marry her she would certainly be a better choice than Isabella! She hoped he would still have room in his heart for her as a friend.

They'd progressed past two houses that were similar to the admiral's, both in the date of construction and style. The plantations surrounding the stately houses were young, allowing the sun to shine fully on the white stone of which they were built, creating a dazzling impression. It reminded her of Bath, but rather a seaside version of that elegant city.

"But now you must tell me why you've been gone so much from Bleadon this last year," George said, reminding Jane of her earlier promise.

"I've been in London for the Season with my Aunt Phoebe," began Jane with a self-deprecating grin, "who, with a missionary zeal, has marched me to each and every soirée, ball and rout we were invited to, and some we were not! I graced the walls of Almack's, curtsied to the Prince Regent, ogled Lord Byron and Lady Caroline from my aunt's opera box in the usual fashion, drove down Rotten Row in a high-perched phaeton with a corinthian of lurid reputation, and danced the waltz with the most dandified tulip of the ton you'd ever hope to see, yet..."

"Yet?" prompted George, her eyes wide with gleeful appreciation of Jane's wit.

"Yet, despite strict adherence to these absurd rituals, I left London at the end of the Season in the unfortunate state in which I'd arrived...unbetrothed and unrepentant!"

"Unrepentant? Whatever do you mean?" cried George.

"My Aunt Phoebe does not know this, and I'm depending on you to keep it a secret between us...." Jane spoke low and leant her head confidingly close, as all the while her eyes danced with mischief. "I received not one, but two very creditable offers of marriage. And I repulsed them both! With all the work my dear aunt went to to expose me to the view of so many worthy gentleman, I should be truly penitent. But I'm not, you see. There you have it!''

''You're so diverting!'' observed George, laughing delightedly at her lively companion's conversation. Then, in a more sober tone, she asked, ''But don't you want to ever marry, Jane? Most girls do.'' *And what about Tony?* she silently wondered. George waited, holding her breath for Jane's answer.

''I want to be married to the right man,'' Jane responded, her voice turned thoughtful and serious. ''I want to marry a man I truly love.''

George was about to ask her outright if the man she truly loved was Tony, but she dared not. Perhaps she was afraid of the answer. While Jane became immersed in a deep study, George's eyes wandered ahead to the approaching vista of a broad, sandy plateau. Two or three buildings stood there, fronted by a wide pavement for walking. They must have been built as lodgings, for in every other window a To Let sign was displayed. On the ground floor of one such building was a subscription library and in another, a confectioner's shop.

''Is this the mall you spoke of?'' George said with some surprise. ''There is more activity later in the day, I suppose,'' she added doubtfully.

''I'm afraid not,'' said Jane. ''The man who owns these buildings ran out of money and enthusiasm before he could create enough interest in the place to make it profitable. A great deal more needs to be built and promoted to attract a steady patronage of loyal visitors. There is an occasional family with whooping cough down from Town who cannot afford the amenities of a real resort, but that certainly is not enough to keep the place going. The confectioner's shop is closed now and the subscription library only opens two days a week. I'm afraid the place will fall into disrepair and these buildings become an eyesore rather than a boon to the village if something is not done soon."

"Surely someone would like to invest in the place? It has a good start," said George encouragingly.

"Those who have money generally have no desire to invest in a seaside resort. And those who would wish to invest in a seaside resort generally have no money! But I suppose anything is possible," she added pensively.

"The view is lovely," offered George. And it was. The plateau rounded gradually, giving an expansive view of the sea. Seagulls dotted the cloudless sky and ...

"Good heavens, isn't that Tony?" But of course it was. There was no mistaking the viscount's tall, straight figure, even at such a distance. George was surprised to discover him out so early in the day. Fashionable gentlemen did not usually present themselves before an advanced hour of the morning, even in the country. And who was that short man in the brown suit standing beside him? And what were they doing standing on that cliff just across the dune? The man in the brown suit had papers in his hand and was pointing at some thing or some place to the left of where she stood with Jane.

"It is Tony, isn't it?" said Jane off handedly. "Out for a walk, I daresay, just as we are!"

"But who is with him?" asked George, her eyes alight with curiosity.

"I haven't a clue!" said Jane, taking George's arm and attempting to turn her round.

"But surely in Bleadon one knows everybody!" George insisted, unwilling to look away from the interesting pair.

Suddenly, and apparently without taking the least notice of Jane and George, the viscount and the stranger retreated and vanished from view.

"How odd!" cried George.

"Yes, but there's no doubt a very reasonable explanation," said Jane dismissively. "Why don't we go back to the house now? I'm famished!"

George agreed to the plan and they turned to retrace their steps down the hill. Having been talked out of her embarrassment by Jane, and having had a meagre dinner the night before, George was quite ravenous herself. And she was rather eager to see Tony, too.

"GOOD NEWS!" exclaimed Lord Sarre, as he sauntered quite late in to the breakfast room, impeccably turned out in a forest-green jacket, buff breeches and tasseled Hessians. Everyone had long since finished eating, but had been lingering over their coffee and hot chocolate as if they didn't quite know what to do without the viscount's enlivening and commanding presence. Isabella had been especially sulky, feeling her only purpose for being in such an insipid little town was to claim his lordship's attention, and then when he hadn't the courtesy to stay at her elbow during all her waking hours she grew waspish in the extreme. Now each head turned towards Lord Sarre, their expressions brightening at the happy tenor of his voice.

"Good news?" Isabella repeated, batting her luxurious eyelashes and thrusting her bosom out to display the daring décolletage she felt compelled to expose since the viscount was not moving fast enough in the courtship to suit her, or her mother.

"We shall be having another visitor," he said cryptically and smiled all round the table at each curious face, lingering a little longer on both Jane's and George's shining countenances. "That is, if my uncle does not object," he amended, turning to fill his plate at the sideboard.

"That would depend upon whom you've invited, Tony," growled the admiral with a twinkle in his eye, quite enjoying the guessing game his nephew had initiated.

"It is a relative, Uncle Jacob."

"That tells me nothing to the point, you young jackanapes! I've so many relatives I don't know the half of them, and the half I know are for the most part damned unpleasant house guests!'' he bellowed, then let out a bark of laughter.

''Now, Uncle,'' began Tony, peering over his shoulder at the older man with a teasing gleam in his eye. ''Who of all our numerous kin do you find so objectionable, pray tell?''

''Most of them! But who've you invited?''

''Is it a man or a woman?'' asked Micah.

''Animal, mineral or vegetable?'' quipped George with a gurgle of laughter.

''Animal, absolutely!'' responded the viscount, his eyes shining back at George as he seated himself next to Isabella.

''Don't tell me you've invited another of your charming cousins?'' purred Isabella venomously, leaning slightly forward so as to secure the viscount the best possible view of her charms and levelling a narrowed look at Jane.

When Jane looked back, all innocence, George's suspicions that Jane rather enjoyed Isabella's frequent attempts to offend her were confirmed. She couldn't help giggling.

''You are in high gig today, Miss Georgiana,'' commented the viscount as he buttered his biscuit and took a bite, completely unconcerned that a roomful of people were watching him eat.

''I am indeed,'' replied George, trying to convey with an earnest look an apology for her missish behaviour of the night before. She must have succeeded, because his responding smile was full of warmth and approval. George felt she could bask forever in the sunshine of such a look, but Micah interrupted.

"Dash it, Tony!" he exclaimed, his patience worn thin. "Out with it! Who the devil—I mean, who the deuce is coming?"

"My brother John is coming," the Viscount answered simply, carving his ham with relish. "At least I hope he shall. I've been writing a letter to him this morning and have just sent Linders into town to post it. That is why I'm so late. Writing letters is a grinding business!"

"But I thought you were late because—" George began, but she stopped in midsentence when Jane squeezed her hand very hard beneath the table. Grimacing expressively, she finished lamely with, "because you overslept."

"George, if you cannot say anything worth hearing, do, for heaven's sake, keep your peace!" admonished Mrs. Lacy. "How long Lord Sarre sleeps is entirely his own business. And why do you grimace so, child? When one is sitting at the table, one should—"

"Don't berate her on my account, Mrs. Lacy," broke in the viscount with a smile belied by the dangerous glint in his eyes. Alarmed by his lordship's hard look, and not understanding it in the least, Mrs. Lacy fell silent.

While the others politely expressed their hopes that John would respond favourably to the invitation extended him, George's heart fluttered with gratitude for the viscount's interruption of her mother's scolding. How kind he was! But also how puzzling! Why hadn't he mentioned his morning's excursion as another reason for his lateness, and why did Jane keep her from asking him about it?

George turned to whisper these questions to Jane, but was stopped short by the complete lack of composure evident in her friend's appearance. Patches of deep rose glowed on Jane's cheeks, her eyes shone softly and lustrously as if she were in the midst of some blissful dream, and one hand trembled visibly as it rested on the table while the other clutched and reclutched a napkin until it lay grotesquely wrinkled in her lap.

"Do we go to the sands then, after I've eaten?" Lord Sarre was saying, seemingly oblivious to the effect his announcement had had on Jane.

"Shouldn't we wait until we've digested our food properly?" said Isabella, wishing to put off the dreaded dip in the sea for as long as possible.

"By the time we've walked to the machines and changed into our bathing clothes, I think we shall have sufficiently digested our breakfast," said the viscount decisively. "Besides," he continued, standing up and tossing his napkin onto the table, "I do so want to see your fine dark eyes all aglow, Miss Lacy, as you rest them on the shining sea. I'm quite sure the sun will pale in comparison." He bowed slightly as he pronounced the grandiose compliment and reached for Isabella's hand, kissing it right there before the lot of them. George's mouth nearly fell open at such a flirtatious display in front of Jane. She really did not understand the viscount's intentions in the least!

However, Isabella's lagging confidence in Lord Sarre's admiration was revived by this contrived bit of flummery, and she smiled and simpered, looking to George for all the world like a plump partridge swelling and puffing its feathers.

Mrs. Lacy smiled benevolently on the affecting scene, but was not emboldened to speak again, still confused by Lord Sarre's earlier set-down over such a trifling thing as her chastisement of George.

"My solicitor is due to arrive this morning," the admiral was saying as he got up from the table, "so I'll be leaving you. But before I go," he added, almost as an afterthought, "I'd best advise you on the choices you'll have as to dippers at the ladies' bathing machines. Mrs. Stone tends to imbibe a little too freely of her medicinal potion, if you catch my meaning. And Mrs. Ford is on a crutch, having sprained her ankle last week. Mrs. Stone may fall asleep and leave you in the drink too long, quite unattended, puckering your skin at the very least, or at worst, allowing you to be sucked out by the tide! Mrs. Ford is excruciatingly slow, finding it uncommonly difficult to use her crutch in the water, and may keep you shivering in your wet clothes for some time before you are supplied with towels. She has a girl from the village to help her, but it's Peg from the Fox and Crown. 'Fraid she's a little short in the sheet. The choice is yours, of course."

"Father!" exclaimed Jane, nudged out of her stupor by these prosaic recommendations. "Why didn't you tell me about Mrs. Ford's sprained ankle? I had settled it to my own satisfaction that Mrs. Stone's bathing machine was out of the question, but now you tell me we shall meet with vexation at Mrs. Ford's as well! Now I don't know what to do!"

"Well, I know what choice I would make between the two," Isabella advised with a superior smug, as if she were imparting wisdom to a simpleton. "I would visit Mrs. Stone."

"And why is that, my dear Miss Lacy?" asked Lord Sarre, evidently still in a mood to humour Isabella with smiling gallantries.

"Because there is nothing so insufferable, in my opinion, as a cripple, limping and knocking about, always on the look-out for sympathy, quite taking advantage of anyone who should show the least concern! Please, I implore you, spare me the likes of Mrs. Ford!" She laughed affectedly, but her cruel humour was received with such astonishment by the others, the laugh soon died in the tomblike stillness which pervaded the room.

George was as appalled as she usually was by Isabella's unfortunate lack of proper feeling. But in this instance her disgust seemed to be shared equally by the others, with the exception of Mrs. Lacy. The admiral's and Micah's eyes were alternately fixed on the floor or the ceiling in embarrassed distress, while Jane had lost her sense of humour where Isabella was concerned and glared at her in an obvious display of fierce dislike.

The smile Lord Sarre had worn disappeared into a mask of angry hauteur as he drew himself up quite stiffly and said, in measured, frozen accents, "Then I fear we shall seriously discommode you, Miss Lacy, when my brother John arrives. He, unfortunately, is a cripple."

The smug expression fell from Isabella's face, leaving it foolishly blank. Mrs. Lacy gasped and clutched her side.

"A Hussar guard in the Ninth Regiment, he lost his right leg just below the knee at the battle of Waterloo." He paused, a bitter smile twisting his handsome face into grim, sardonic lines. "But I always strove to keep John from the mire of self-pity by reminding him with what bravery he sacrificed himself for the benefit of all the good people of England, people like me and you, Miss Lacy." Then, turning neatly on his heel, the viscount left the room without another word.

Tension enveloped the remaining company like an evil fog, and did not dissipate even after Micah, the admiral and Jane filed out in a silent procession, leaving only Mrs. Lacy, Isabella and George. George's heart ached for the pain she was sure both parties were feeling in the situation. Though Isabella had uttered some truly unkind remarks, George felt sure she had not meant them and was only trying, in a misguided fashion, to be clever. And as for Tony, she felt his hurt as surely as if it had been her own! To have a beloved brother who had fought valiantly in the War, been wounded and suffered still, made mock of even in an indirect manner would be horrible.

"Oh, Isabella, Isabella! I shall swoon!" announced Mrs. Lacy faintly as she continued to clutch her side and breathe rapidly. "I fear you have nipped his ardour in the bud with your sharp tongue! What a pretty botch this is!"

"How was I to know his brother was a cripple?" Isabella defended herself petulantly and snapped her fan open, plying it with energy through the air in an effort to cool her burning cheeks.

"Perhaps if you refrained from unkind comments about people in general, Isabella, you would not find yourself in such a pickle. You never know who you may be offending," George advised in a quiet, sober voice.

"Oh stuff, George! Next I suppose you shall be quoting from the *Christian Comforter!* Spare me the sermon, if you please!" Isabella snapped back.

"You'll never bring him up to scratch now, my dear," Mrs. Lacy predicted with melancholy conviction. "We may as well pack!"

"Pray, Mama, do *not* remind me of this unlucky mistake when once we are home!" Isabella warned her mother as she stood up to leave the room. "I daresay Lord Sarre is far too sensitive about a mere joke, anyway!"

"But he *is* a viscount, my angel," wailed Mrs. Lacy, staggering to her feet in a state of profound agitation.

"Is this the only regret the two of you have?" exclaimed George. "That you have failed to bamboozle Lord Sarre into marriage? What of *his* feelings?"

"You are always ready to sympathize with everyone except your own sister, George," spat Mrs. Lacy, her eyes as hard and black as jet. "Your thoughts and opinions are worthless in this case, young lady. You know nothing about—"

But George had heard enough. Obviously her concern for Isabella's feelings were unnecessary, since her elder sister apparently felt no remorse for her unkind words and only regretted them insofar as they had deprived her of nabbing a title. Completely disgusted, and unable to turn her usual deaf ear to her mother's unfair remonstrations, she gave them each a pained look and quit the room.

LORD SARRE PACED the beach with a vengeance, insensible to the sandy scratches incurred by his gleaming Hessians, which Linders had blackened so lovingly with champagne. The meanness of Miss Isabella Lacy's small mind never ceased to amaze him! Each day revealed her as more selfish and thoughtless than the day before! He could not conceive how George had remained so unpolluted with such an example as her mother and older sister to go by!

"Tony! Wish you would slow down! Dash it if it ain't hard enough keeping up with you, much less holding conversation!" complained Micah between heaving breaths.

"I don't want to talk, Micah!" growled the viscount. "You might as well go back to the house!"

"That's cutting a wheedle if ever I heard one!" puffed Micah, his forehead beginning to drip with perspiration. "Got to talk about it. Got to decide what to do, dash it! What about George?"

The viscount ceased his pacing and frowned down at the tips of his boots in deep concentration. "Yes, what about George?" he muttered, as if to himself.

Micah took advantage of this welcome interruption of frenzied movement to pluck an embroidered handkerchief from the pocket of his pantaloons and mop his brow. "Overheard Mrs. Lacy say they might as well pack. They'll be gone in a trice if you don't smooth over this tiff with Isabella. Goes against the grain, I know, but what's to do?"

"You expect me to apologize to that...that witch!" the viscount fairly shouted at his friend. "She ought to apologize to me!" He resumed his pacing. Micah sighed, tucked away the handkerchief and fell into step behind him.

"Agreed, Tony! But wouldn't call her a witch, precisely! Just unthinking, y'know. But unless you're prepared to court George properly, you must still play the flirt with Isabella! And even if you do secure George's affections, won't do at all to be on the outs with her family! Isabella will be your sister, Tony! And that...and Mrs. Lacy your mother! Think on it, Tony!"

Micah had said his piece and was now resolved to quit treading the beach like a hungry gull on the lookout for a morsel washed in by the sea. He glanced around for somewhere to sit, but was obliged to stand, having no wish to incur the wrath of his valet by sullying the seat of his breeches.

Lord Sarre continued his pacing for a minute or two, then stopped suddenly and faced Micah. "Got me leg-shackled to George already, have you?" he challenged in a low, angry voice. "Do you suppose me so ready to throw my cap over the windmill for a chit plagued by such a family? Do you imagine me so far gone to reason that I would pant after a girl who doesn't show the least inclination to return my warmer sentiments, and only wants to be my friend?"

Micah returned the viscount's fierce gaze unwaveringly and simply replied, "Don't try to gammon *me*, Tony. Know it's all April and May with you. Written all over you, don't you know?"

Lord Sarre's frown increased momentarily, then he let out a huge breath, releasing in one giant puff all the frustration several days of play-acting had built up inside him. The chiselled lines of anger that marked his handsome face melted away as if by magic as he eased himself down onto the ground and sat cross-legged in the sand. With his eyes fixed on the sea, he asked in a weary voice, "Is it so obvious?"

Micah eyed the grainy surface upon which his friend had chosen to seat his elegant form and mentally weighed the luxury of resting his tired legs against the sure knowledge that Bennett, his austere valet, would be miffed to discover his clothes encrusted with sand. Deciding in favour of his present comfort, he sat down beside the viscount.

"To *me* it's obvious, Tony. But I've seen you around cartloads of woman—light skirts, Cyprians, lusty widows, bored wives and even the season's latest Incomparable! Never saw you look at any of 'em as you look at George! But you needn't fear that the others know. Don't think they know you like I do, 'cept maybe Jane. S'pose you'll convince the chit that you'll do as a husband?"

"I need time, Micah, just a little more time. I don't think she's indifferent to me, but she's so green I suspect she doesn't understand half the feelings she has. And I don't want to scare her away by rushing the business." He sighed again, but this time with a bemused smile curving his mouth and lighting his green eyes. "I don't even know precisely why I'm so taken with the girl, Micah. But I'll be damned if I don't mean to marry her!"

"Then, dear fellow, better start thinking of some pretty words for Isabella," advised Micah sagely. "No need to grovel. Just enough to keep her and her mother in Bleadon while you convince George that she's smitten!"

"I'll do it!" replied the viscount, his eyes hardening as he contemplated the loathsome necessity of approaching Isabella. Then, remembering earlier conversations with Micah on the subject, he said, "I thought you were opposed to my using Isabella to further my acquaintance with George, Micah. You've changed your tune!"

"Not really," objected Micah with a troubled frown. "Still feel the same way, but I promised my assistance in exchange for the greys and I don't go back on my word! B'sides, see how it is with you and George! Got to get the two of you together, somehow. But do it quickly, will you? I still think Mrs. Lacy is capable of trying to trick you, and . . . and— dash it, Tony!—can't help but feel we're treating Isabella shabbily by leading her on this way!"

"No need to worry about Isabella, Micah," replied his friend. "I don't believe she has a heart to break!"

"Used to," muttered Micah.

"Well, you may be the better judge of that," Lord Sarre admitted, "since you've known her longer. But so far I've seen no evidence of its existence!"

Micah did not reply.

"When do you think I should smooth things over?" said his lordship briskly, bringing the conversation back to its original course. "This evening before dinner would be best, I think. See if you can ascertain whether they mean to leave today or tomorrow, and if they are decided upon leaving today you must somehow convince them to stay longer. By dinner I hope I shall have dredged up enough false civility to placate them into staying. Though I shall hate myself for it," he coolly added. "Besides, since the sea bathing scheme is put off for now, I'll attend to some business in town that could keep me occupied for the better part of the day.''

"Tony, I begin to think you've a mistress in each town or that you transport one with you wherever you go!" exclaimed Micah, his face expressing a kind of reluctant admiration. "When you speak of business in Bath and now in Bleadon, what else can I suppose? Only business I've ever known you to concern yourself with has had to do with your estates!''

"I haven't a mistress in Bath or Bleadon, or anywhere for that matter,'' returned the viscount dryly. "I haven't had for some time. No one has been able to catch my fancy for an age, till now. . . .'' The bemused smile returned to soften his expression and send him off on a daydream, the contents of which Micah could only guess at.

Considerably embarrassed, Micah stood up and dusted off his breeches as best he could. "Going in, Tony,'' he mumbled. "Change my clothes, y'know!''

"Thank you again, Micah!" said the Viscount, reaching forth a hand to shake. "For everything!''

"S'nothing, Tony,'' replied Micah with a shy smile and a blink.

CHAPTER SIX

IT WAS AN ODD DAY all round for George. The various people residing in Neptune House skulked through its halls in the earnest endeavour of avoiding one another, or stayed in their rooms. Despite the admiral's polite (but not very pressing) note to his guests that they might join him in the dining hall for nuncheon, Mrs Lacy declined on behalf of herself and her two daughters, claiming a sort of group indisposition. George wanted more than anything to accept the admiral's invitation, but Mrs. Lacy (perhaps recognizing how much George wanted to go, and afraid lest she say something to the admiral of which Mrs. Lacy would disapprove) forbade her to do so. Therefore, the servants were kept busy distributing trays to bedchambers and supplying Mrs. Lacy with vial after vial of lavender water. Feeling much too overpowered by the untoward events of the morning for the tiring inconveniences of an extended coach ride, Mrs. Lacy had settled it that they would not begin their journey to Bath until the morrow. She would inform the admiral of her decision later in the day.

While George reluctantly obeyed her mother about dining with the admiral, she escaped Mrs. Lacy's bedchamber (where she had been ordered to sit since mid-morning) when that lady finally succumbed to a laudanum-induced slumber, and began to look about for other occupants of the house. Since she had no desire to avoid anyone, George presented herself regularly in the main rooms and skirted the outside of the building frequently in the hope of encountering Tony, Jane or the admiral, or even Micah. To the former three she wanted to apologize for her sister's unfeeling remarks, and with Micah she hoped to have a heart-to-heart talk like the ones they used to have as children.

The awkwardly executed attentions Micah had for some reason been compelled to pay her in Bath had thankfully diminished considerably since their arrival in Bleadon, and his manners had returned to the former comfortable incivility of before. This change in his behaviour had encouraged George to hope that he'd seen the folly of the ridiculous notion he'd taken into his head about courting her. Right now, more than anything, she wanted a friend to talk to. With Tony and Jane upset, and rightfully so, Micah seemed the only one who might fit into that category.

So it was with great pleasure that she bumped into him as she rounded a corner during one of her rotations of the house. Deep in thought and startled to see someone after seeing nobody all day, she quite literally did bump into him, her forehead impacting squarely with his chin and sending them both sprawling with surprising force to the ground. After the initial shock had worn off, each acquired the unwelcome knowledge of how damp the grass could be even in the heat of midafteroon.

"Good gad, George! Now you've done it!" exclaimed Micah, who'd scampered to his feet and was craning his neck to observe the large green smudge that clung to the seat of his white pantaloons. "I've just endured the wrathful silence of Bennett for the sand in my buff breeches, and now, just because you do not look where you're going, I'm to be chastised for yet another change of clothes before dinner!"

"You're as much at fault as I!" retorted George, rubbing her forehead and glaring at Micah. "But then you were always one to pass the blame when we were growing up, though we were both involved in some prank or other!" She struggled to her feet without Micah's assistance.

"I suppose you were not to blame for letting loose Squire Bromley's prize pig and hiding it in the woods in that wretched pen you made me build?" returned Micah, resting his fists on his hips and thrusting his face to within an inch or two of George's. "I should not have even thought to do it if you had not begged me to help you!"

"Micah, you were as sorry as I was to discover Petunia to be destined for the squire's larder! You agreed that we were duty-bound to rescue her from such a horrid end!"

"We were found out anyway, George, and Petunia ended as an Easter ham and several rashers of bacon, as I recall! And didn't you eat some of that bacon when the squire sent it over as a peace offering after your mother had reddened your bottom with a pussy willow stick?''

"Oh, how unkind of you to remind me of it!" wailed George, covering her face to hide the beginnings of a smile. "I did not know I was eating Petunia, and I wasn't able to stomach pork for several months after, if you remember!"

"Nor I," fairly shouted Micah, enjoying the altercation with all the zest of a ten-year-old boy. "Because *my* punishment was that I was forbidden to eat pork for an entire half year!"

By now it was impossible for George to suppress her enjoyment of such a delightful memory, and she burst into laughter. Micah joined her and they turned with one accord to walk round the back of the house together, their arms companionably linked and smiles wreathing their faces.

"You're a sad little ninnyhammer," observed Micah affectionately.

"And you're the biggest looby!" returned George with an equal amount of responding warmth.

After exchanging these amiable opinions, they both fell silent, each absorbed in the subject they wished to broach with the other. George spoke first.

"Micah, I've been wanting to talk to you about your sudden interest in me of late...."

"But George, you know I've always been interested in you!" objected Micah, wilfully misunderstanding her and beginning to blink.

"You know precisely what I mean!" declared George. "And I think I've waited long enough for an explanation, especially since you seem finally to have come to your senses!"

George watched Micah as he appeared to be struggling with a decision. She hoped it meant he was going to tell her the truth, but, then again, he could be concocting a Banbury tale.

"George," he finally blurted out, "if I had not made such a fuss and got your mother to bring you out, you wouldn't even be on this trip, y'know!"

George's eyes grew wide. "Do you mean you pretended to be calf-eyed over me just to allow me more freedom?"

"Well, er, yes! That's true enough. Exactly so!" he exclaimed emphatically.

"That was very kind of you, Micah," said George, much struck by the idea that her old playmate had had the urge to think of her at all. "But why, for heaven's sake, didn't you confide your plans to *me?* I was so mortified by your silly speeches I thought I'd die!"

"Dash it, George, would you have co-operated?"

This question made George thoughtful. After a moment, she responded, "I suppose not! I was content as I was. I did not know being out would afford me as much pleasure as it does."

Micah smiled. "Having a good time, then?"

"Until this morning," said George gloomily. "Now I expect we shall have to return to Bath!"

"Your mother is determined to go?" asked Micah, thankful to be afforded an introduction to the subject he wanted to discuss without being obvious about it.

"Yes!"

"Today?"

"No, tomorrow."

"Then I should not worry if I were you," said Micah with such confidence George eyed him suspiciously.

"Why not?"

"Well, er..." began Micah, blinking repeatedly. "Think Tony will smooth things over."

"You really think so?" exclaimed George, her whole expression brightening at the possibility.

"Know so!" Micah assured her.

"But why should Tony tolerate Isabella's disposition when he doesn't really have to?" George wondered aloud. "He isn't related to her or anything! I can hardly keep from quarrelling with her myself and she's my sister!"

Micah remained silent, allowing George to draw whatever conclusion she must to explain the enigma. It went sorely against the grain to keep her in the dark as to the viscount's real feelings towards the various members of her family, including herself, but he was honour-bound to support Tony in this deuced charade and could only hope all would be well in the end.

"There's a great deal going on round here that I don't understand, Micah," George admitted, remembering Jane's behaviour at the breakfast table. Then, recalling that Tony had said he'd been writing a letter to his brother John that morning rather than roaming the cliffs as he'd actually been doing, and half suspecting John to be a figment of the viscount's fertile imagination, she asked, "Have you ever met this brother of Tony's, Micah?"

"Yes, before he lost his leg. Lively fellow! Always up to some rig or other! But Tony tells me he's very different now. Hope he doesn't put a damper on things! Not sure why Tony sent for 'im!"

They walked steadily on and were now approaching the front of the house again. "Where's that shaggy mutt of yours?" Micah asked suddenly. "Used to follow you everywhere, George. Drowned in the sea?"

"Of course not, Micah," replied George calmly. "The truth is, Whiskers now allots his time between me and Mrs. Higgens, the cook. The servants are kinder and more generous here than at Lacy manor, and Cook took a liking to Whiskers and he to her."

"Fickle little beast! Just like a woman!" observed Micah rather more feelingly than the occasion warranted.

"Oh, no, Micah!" exclaimed George, defending her pet. "After all, what dog could resist giblet gravy and meaty bones freely given throughout the day? I expect he shall grow as fat and happy as Mrs. Higgens before we leave this place!"

Micah chuckled, but became sober and thoughtful almost immediately. After a long pause, he said, "Haven't spent much time round Isabella since I was in short pants, y'know, George, but can't help but see she grows more like your mother by the day."

"Pity, isn't it?" agreed George.

"Indeed!" replied Micah grimly.

This sobering thought propelled them both into a brown study which lasted several minutes. Finally Micah seemed to shake himself and said, "Won't mind if I have to pay you a compliment or two just to keep your mother's hopes up, will you George? Best to remind her from time to time why she's allowed you to come along! Wouldn't put it past the old . . . your mother to send you home on the post otherwise."

"Well, all right," George agreed reluctantly. "But mind you do not fawn or act loverlike, or I swear I shall grow quite violently ill!" she warned him, her blue eyes flashing.

"Never!" Micah exclaimed, deeply affronted. "Assure you, George, though it were only play-acting, making love to you would make me ill, too! Might even turn up my toes!"

Charmed by these pleasing expressions, and feeling the great good luck of having a friend who so closely shared her own way of thinking, George smiled up at Micah and they walked into the house quite in harmony with each other.

THE RHYTHMIC TICKING of the ornate ormolu clock on the black marble mantelpiece could be plainly heard throughout the silent drawing-room. George sat with her hands fidgeting in her lap as she waited for the same thing they all waited for: Lord Sarre's appearance in the room. The admiral had his meals served with military punctuality, and it now lacked only five minutes until the dinner hour.

Glancing over at her mother and Isabella, George marvelled that they had presented themselves at all. When George informed them that the viscount meant to smooth over the morning's tiff, neither of the ladies would grant her the least credibility. George applied to Micah for assistance, and though they were loath to feel an obligation to their insignificant neighbour for such gratifying news, they could not deny that Micah must surely know what he was talking about. All in a flutter, Isabella dressed with more care than usual, donning a shockingly daring gown of jonquil silk, more suited for a ballroom than a simple country supper.

Jane had entered the room only moments before and looked at Isabella's inappropriate gown with barely contained disgust, distantly wishing her and Mrs. Lacy a good evening and saving her genuine smile for her father, Micah and George. But despite the pleasure which George derived from Jane's smile and the guarded hope that she was not included in Jane's anger towards the Lacys, no conversation was forthcoming from the young lady. Jane sat pensively staring out the window at the lawn.

The admiral declined to converse as well, but George did not think his reluctance to speak sprang from the same source as Jane's. He'd informed them earlier that his big toe was inflamed and he'd no doubt that a large storm was brewing off the coast of England and would be descending on their humble village within a week's time. George found this information interesting and a little alarming, but Isabella and Mrs. Lacy exchanged looks of patent disbelief and shrugged.

George had, by mere chance, placed herself in such a position that she could see the hallway outside the drawing-room door by the reflection of a large mirror that hung on the wall, and she found herself continually glancing in that direction to watch for Tony's arrival. When the clock began to strike the hour of seven, suspense grew heavy amongst the gathered party. On the third strike, George perceived Tony's image in the mirror. Her heart leapt with fearful and happy anticipation: fear for the awkwardness of his first meeting with Isabella, and happiness because she had longed to see him all day!

Pausing outside the door, the viscount appeared to be straightening his neckcloth and schooling his sober expression into an acceptably pleasant one. Just as the last stroke reverberated through the room, and most of the faces present had fallen in disappointment or chagrin, Tony sauntered in.

"Uncle! Linders tells me we must expect some wretched weather! Is it your respected big toe, or the less reliable knee joint to which we owe this enlightening piece of information, pray tell?" he teased his uncle in a jocular voice, pumping his arm in a hearty handshake.

"It's my big toe, nephew! And you needn't be so flippant about it! Mark my words, we'll be lucky to avoid a hurricane if the fury of the storm is equal to the strength of my discomfort," he gruffly informed them all, turning to accentuate this dire prediction with an ominous lowering of his ponderous brow.

"How do you do, Miss Lacy, Mrs. Lacy?" the viscount was now saying as he bent gracefully over the women's outstretched hands. Mrs. Lacy's face wore a meek, hopeful expression, but Isabella had already decided that Lord Sarre must be completely in her power if he could so readily revert to his old self after delivering such a set-down only hours before.

"You're not angry with me, Lord Sarre?" she suggested with an arch look. Breath was suspended in the room while everyone waited for the viscount's reply. George could observe his face in profile and detected a muscle in his jaw tighten during a pause of perhaps thirty seconds. Then, in a carefully controlled voice and with a horridly polite little smile, he said, "I was hasty in taking offense this morning, Miss Lacy. I realized later that you were only making a joke."

A perfectly tasteless one, thought George, grimacing as she watched the viscount make an apology when
he should rather be the recipient of one.

"I hope we may put this episode firmly behind us
and go on as before," he finished and kissed her hand.

While Isabella smugly forgave him, and Mrs. Lacy's
humble expression faded away, Jane sat seething in her
chair. When Lord Sarre then turned to greet his
cousin, she gave him a look designed to wither. Taking this condemnation in stride, and with a pained
expression only briefly fleeting across his handsome
face, he turned to George.

George did not understand the viscount in the least.
He seemed at one moment to be enamoured of his
cousin and was the next moment spouting silly
professions of admiration for her sister. He'd proven
himself an accomplished liar and had witnessed an
affair (the infamous sea bath) which had caused
George a degree of mortification she hoped never to
endure again. But somehow she could not help but
forgive him all and grant him every benefit of the
doubt. Perhaps, as Jane had said this morning on their
walk, the viscount was a truly forgiving and understanding man and had exercised these charming traits
to Isabella's benefit.

So, how was she to behave towards such a paragon
of virtue (who, along with this recommendation, had
the finest shoulders and the most elegant pair of legs
she'd ever seen) other than to admire his benevo-
lence, (and the excellent cut of his coat), and approve

whatever he did! Smiling radiantly up into his face, she said, "How do you do, Lord Sarre? Have you had a pleasant day?"

"Is it enough to say that it improves by the moment?" he answered in a low voice, out of earshot of the others, and smiling in the most infectious manner. Then in a louder voice, "You must prepare Whiskers for the worst, Miss Georgiana. I believe we will have thunder and lightning in abundance in short order. Uncle Jacob's big toe is always precise to a pin!"

A discussion of the weather thus ensued, joined with spirit by everyone except Jane who seemed still to resent Isabella's remarks of the morning and the viscount's easy dismissal of them. Micah interrupted frequently with comments and questions about Lord Sarre's clothes. Was that jacket by Weston, and who did he prefer more, Stultz or Weston? Was that an Oriental or a Mailcoach he'd created out of his snowy-white neckcloth, and how many of them had he ruined before achieving success? Why did his hair have such an easy wave at the brow while Micah could no more tame his own red hair than tame a bull?

The admiral was willing enough to postpone dinner as long as his big toe was the main meat for discussion, but fripperish gabble was not sufficient inducement to keep him from his mutton. When they were seated at the table, George indulged a freakish whim, which had unaccountably come over her, to stare at the viscount.

Soft candlelight illuminated the table and gleamed off the crystal and silver with brilliant effect. The soft lighting not only presented the table setting to its best advantage, but seemed to enhance the viscount's vital presence as well. Always impeccably groomed, his lordship looked especially well turned out that evening. His royal-blue jacket hugged his wide shoulders without producing the least pull of fabric to detract from the overall effect. His neckcloth was intricate, but in good taste, and his shirt points, though fashionably high, still allowed him ample freedom to turn his head at will. A single pearl pin and signet ring were his only ornaments.

Indeed, such a vigorous-looking man would be rendered ridiculous by an ostentatious display of jewellery. Why, the simpler his attire, thought George, the more attractive such a man would appear! Squire Bromley had always preened himself on being the local fashion plate, but when George mentally compared the two men, the squire's pudgy, bejewelled appearance was clownish compared to the viscount's unpretentious elegance. Brought forcefully to her mind was a vision of Squire Bromley's pantaloons, stretched mercilessly over ponderous thighs, with little rolls of fat squeezed into creases at the knees. Tony's legs must be pure muscle, because she could not recall a single crease in the line of his pantaloons, only nice, smooth lengths of sinew and . . .

Blushing furiously, George was horrified at the path her thoughts had taken! Searching the viscount's face guiltily for any indication that he'd somehow read her mind, she unwittingly drew his attention. He'd been laughing at something his uncle said, his black hair full and luxurious in the candlelight, his straight teeth glinting white, his eyes crinkled into smiling crescents of emerald green, and that deep cleft in his chin begging to be touched and explored... But now he returned her gaze questioningly, his eyes grown liquid and rimmed in grey, his lips, in repose, curving in a faint smile. She imagined that he held his mouth just so when asleep and enjoying a pleasant dream.

"Have your wits gone abegging, child," came her mother's shrill recall to reality. "Do you want the veal or not?"

"Yes, I suppose I do," George stammered, dropping her head to stare at the empty plate in front of her and reaching for a tumbler to quench her suddenly parched throat. But trembling hands frequently do not perform well, and the glass slipped through her fingers just as she was about to take a sip, spilling the iced lemonade all over the front of her blue muslin gown.

Though her bodice was not thoroughly enough soaked to render it transparent, the resemblance between tonight's soaking and yesterday's sea bath were too painfully obvious for George to ignore. As she leapt to her feet in a tumble of confused thoughts and feelings, she glanced at her mother, dreading the inevitable scolding. But while her mother narrowed her eyes and opened her mouth in preparation for just such a purpose, she appeared to have a change of heart when she encountered the viscount's fulminating glare.

This further proof of the viscount's kindness served only to heighten George's embarrassment. "Excuse me, so clumsy..." she stuttered in the general direction of the admiral. "I'd best go and change." She then flew from the room with what she was sure all present must consider unseemly and unladylike speed. But feeling as foolish as she did, she was sure more time spent in the dining hall would only result in some greater disaster, and heaven knew that would be the outside of enough.

SOMEHOW GEORGE GOT THROUGH supper and the rest of the evening, but by the time the piquet table had broken up and Isabella's pianoforte performance had been duly exclaimed over, she was more than ready to retire to her bedchamber. Jane had exerted herself to put George at her ease after her latest accident, and though George appreciated her concern, it was getting rather tiring always to be the recipient of such sympathetic kindness!

The most remarkable occurrence of the evening was the lack of any chastisement from her mother. But even a simpleton could have discovered the reason for Mrs. Lacy's silent tongue. Each time her demeanour suggested she might be about to reprimand George, the viscount levelled such a keen, hard eye upon her, that she didn't dare to open her mouth. The ludicrous look on her mother's face at having to curtail a habit she'd long indulged made George sorely tempted to laugh, but she dared not. The viscount could not always be there to protect her!

After closing her bedchamber door, George sat down at the dressing-table and removed the ivory combs Perkins had placed in her hair before dinner. She brushed out the curls 'til they danced about her ears and rioted in springy ringlets to just above her shoulders in the back. The sea air made her hair rather more difficult to manage, as the natural curls were increasingly inclined to have their own way with each succeeding day. Putting the brush down, she rose and removed her dressing-gown from the armoire, laying it on the bed and smoothing the soft lawn material in an absent-minded fashion, her mind filled with the people and happenings of the last few days.

Feeling restless now that she was away from the oppressiveness of the drawing-room, she moved to the French doors which opened onto the balcony, unlatched them and stepped out. It was a glorious evening. The amethyst sea stretched out below a star-spangled sky, the waves swelling and cresting to their own compelling rhythm. The foaming peaks were laced with moonlight and the sea shells shimmered like gold dust on the sand. The salty breeze was warm and breathed the promise of another cloudless sky on the morrow. She closed her eyes and lifted her face to the delicate caress of moon-fingers on her skin.

"'But soft! What light through yonder window breaks?'"

George was startled to hear Tony's deep, clear voice drifting upwards from the shadowed shrubberies below. She couldn't help but smile and laugh, and leaning over the balcony rails whispered back in tragic accents, "'Oh, Romeo, Romeo, wherefore art thou Romeo?'"

"'It is the east, and Juliet is the sun!'" Tony continued, stepping away from the shadows to reveal himself. He was looking very much as he had the first time George had seen him by the stream: his jacket discarded along with his neckcloth and waistcoat, and his white ruffled shirt open at the throat. Striking a theatrical pose with one opened palm balanced affectedly in front of his chest and the other raised above his head, he crooned, "'Arise, fair sun, and kill the envious moon, who is already sick and pale with grief, that thou her maid art far more fair than she!'"

"Oh, you do it so well!" exclaimed George, clapping her hands in delight. "I daresay you ought to be treading the boards! In no time at all people would be flocking to the theatre to see Braithwaite rather than Kean!"

"I've no intention of usurping that noble thespian as first man of the stage, and I'd not be able to do it even if I tried!" Tony retorted. "Now come down here, George, I've a mind to talk to you tonight!"

"That sounds like a command, Tony," George objected coyly.

"If you continued to argue with me, someone will doubtless hear us before long. Meet me by the edge of the cliff. I'll be waiting." Then, without further ado, he disappeared.

George glanced over at the balconies, which she had learned connected to Jane's and the admiral's bed-chambers. The doors were closed, a fact she was thankful for and which she'd not had the presence of mind to discover earlier, so caught up was she in Tony's playful rendition of one of Shakespeare's more beautiful tragedies. As for Isabella and her mother, neither of them slept with the the windows open, as they supposed that the night air induced premature wrinkling.

George was racked with indecision. She wanted to join Tony outside, but she was fully aware of how reprehensible such behaviour would appear to any-one with the least scruples. And if she were discov-ered slipping out to meet him, it would be assumed that they were lovers; at least it was always so in the novels she'd read! And would they believe her if she told them that she and Tony were only friends?

Her conscience dutifully presented the unwiseness of such a scheme, but in the end her conscience was forcefully suppressed. She wanted to talk to Tony as freely as she had done at their first meeting and there had been no opportunity to do so until tonight. Be-sides, she meant to quiz him about that Banbury tale he'd concocted to explain his lateness at the breakfast table. Throwing a shawl over the rose-sprigged gown of French crepe (her third change of clothes since breakfast) she left the room and tiptoed down the hall, following the same route Jane had shown her that first day.

Passing by the opened kitchen door, she observed Whiskers asleep on a braided rag rug placed lovingly near the dying embers of the cooking fire. However, when she turned the knob and gently pushed the door open, the tiny squeak which emanated from the unoiled hinges woke him up. Tail wagging and small black eyes sparkling beneath his scraggly bangs, Whiskers was ready to go. George could not deny him without the risk of bringing on a barking frenzy, so allowed him to follow her out the door.

Tony was waiting at the beginning of the trail which led down the cliff to the sands. "Here you are at last!" he complained good-naturedly. "Come, take my hand and I'll help you down. I've a lantern, but I dare not light it until we're round the corner."

George gave the viscount her hand and he slowly guided her the first few feet down the path until they were no longer in danger of being seen from the house. Then, setting the lantern on the ground, he stooped to light it, the flame building from a sputtering spark to a golden pool that seemed to envelop them in a cozy, private world of their own.

When the viscount reached again for George's hand, she said, "No, you'd better carry Whiskers, or he'll most certainly trip us up along the way! And I shall place my hand on your back, Tony," she suggested in a shy, little voice, remembering how she'd envied

Jane's doing so the day before. "Only walk slowly, if you please."

He obeyed her without question, and since she could not observe the expression on his face, felt less embarrassment in pressing her small hand against his muscled back for support. In this manner they descended the hill and arrived on the beach without injury, where she reluctantly removed her hand and wondered why she had enjoyed the contact so thoroughly. Tony placed Whiskers on the ground, saying, "There, you little ragamuffin! Stay out of the water!"

"Well, we're here," stated George quite unnecessarily, twining her fingers together and swinging them self-consciously in the air. "You said you wanted to talk to me," she reminded him.

"So I do, but must it necessarily be about something in particular?" he teased her, raising the lantern at a level with her face.

"Well I've something particular to say to *you*," she informed him with a look of mock reproval.

"Should I be unnerved, Miss Georgiana?" he asked her, raising a black brow. The glow from the lantern shed light on only half the viscount's face, and with his brow lifted in that devilish way, George received a most unsettling impression: he seemed to resemble a satyr. But her fascinated stare must have amused him because suddenly he smiled, the wicked image happily dissolving in the night air.

"I suspect you *should* be unnerved, but I daresay you are so hardened at the art of spinning whiskers...."

"Spinning whiskers, George?" The viscount feigned shock.

"...and telling farradiddles of the most reprehensible nature!"

"Except for the time I did not tell you precisely who I was, George, I don't ever recall..."

"What about this morning, if you please?"

"This morning?" he repeated blankly.

"When you explained that you were late to breakfast because you were writing a letter," persisted George, a little impatient with the viscount's innocent act.

"I *was* writing a letter!" he protested.

"But earlier we saw you walking on the cliffs...."

"Who is *we,* poppet?"

"Jane and I. And you were with some gentleman that Jane didn't recognize," George said. "I thought perhaps *he* had detained you. Then when Jane stopped me from asking you about it at the table, I began to wonder why it was necessary to keep it a secret."

"Let's walk down the beach a little way, George, shall we? Here, take my arm. I'll hold the lantern thusly."

George allowed the viscount to tuck her arm snugly against his side while he dangled the lantern from his other elbow, but though she quite enjoyed the friendly gesture she wasn't to be distracted from her purpose.

"Well?" she asked him now.

"Yes, George, you did see me out walking this morning," Tony finally answered seriously. "But it is still quite true that I wrote a letter. Both activities kept me from an early breakfast."

"Who was that man? He held papers in his hand, I noticed. What were they? And why did Jane crush my hand beneath the table when I—" Suddenly realizing that her questions were impertinent, George said, "Oh, I beg your pardon! These things are none of my business! It's just that I've such a wondrous..."

"...large curiosity," Tony finished for her and they both laughed. "Don't apologize! I wish I *could* tell you what I was doing this morning," he added vaguely. "But I can't. At least, not yet."

George was disappointed. She was unhappily reminded of when they'd first met and he'd given her only part of his name, requesting that she be satisfied with that until a later time.

Seeming to read her thoughts, he said, "It's not the same as when I withheld my identity from you. That was a whimsical start of mine. This other situation involves some very important and pressing considerations, and has to do with the future and welfare of someone very..."

Even in the darkness George could see that he was in the grip of some stirring emotion.

"Don't go on!" she cried, grasping his upper arm in an impulsive gesture. "You needn't tell me anything, you know! I'm a sad meddle!"

Tony remained silent. George was kicking herself for having made her friend uncomfortable and was determined to remedy her mistake. "I do so enjoy Bleadon, don't you?" she exclaimed with enthusiasm, hoping to introduce a painless topic, while her mind reeled with all the possibilities implied by his words and the emotion behind them.

"I've always been fond of the place," Tony agreed, following George's lead. "John and I spent time here almost every summer while we were growing up. And even after we'd gone on to school, many of our holidays were spent here. John especially loved it. He and Jane are of an age, you know, and how they used to carry on! Jane was the worst little hoyden you've ever clapped eyes on in those days! The two of them were always up to some mischief or other."

Seeing an opportunity to do something she'd wanted to do all day, George regretfully abandoned her resolve to avoid touchy subjects and said, "As you are speaking of your brother, Tony, might I beg your forgiveness for my sister's thoughtless words this morning? She did not mean to..."

"Don't apologize for Isabella, George," the viscount interrupted warmly. "*You* are not to blame for her thoughtlessness, and *she* cannot seem to help herself," he ended matter-of-factly. "You must know that I'm particularly sensitive about my brother, in any case. I have this wretched awareness that if I'd been the younger son, it would have been I on the battlefield and not John!"

"Tony, you don't mean to say you feel at fault for John losing his leg, do you?" cried George, aghast at the possibility that he might entertain such a distorted view of things.

"No, I'm not such a gull as that. Only, I feel for him exceedingly, you see. He isn't taking it well at all. I want to help him if I can."

"I'm sure you will!" said George feelingly and with such confidence in her voice that the viscount found himself hard-pressed not to take her in his arms right then and there, crush her to him and declare himself the happiest man in the world. Suppressing these urges with no little difficulty, he determined to celebrate the buoyant feelings she'd unwittingly unleashed in his jaded soul and thwart his more amorous inclinations by teasing her mercilessly.

"I've changed my mind about you, George," he said in a mock serious tone.

"What do you mean?" George stopped walking and stood smiling up at him, pleasantly startled by his abrupt change of mood.

"I'm still convinced you're a magical creature of some sort, but not an elf or a faerie, or even—alas!— a nymph!"

"What, then?" she demanded, giggling.

"You're a leprechaun!"

"How so? Do I look like a leprechaun?"

Lord Sarre lifted the lantern above George's head. The light streamed down on her golden hair, picking out a sun-streaked curl or two to shine rather more than the rest, her blue eyes sparkled with happiness, and the rose-sprigged gown moved gently in the warm breeze, moulding itself to the curves of her trim figure. "No, you do not!" he answered emphatically.

"Then why...?"

"Because—sprite!—I've a strong suspicion that if someone were to catch you, you'd present them, albeit reluctantly, with a pot of gold!"

Completely overwhelmed by such an enigmatic declaration, and feeling rather alarmed by Tony's glittering green eyes and strange smile, she swallowed nervously and suggested that they return to the house.

"Of course," said the viscount quite composedly, lowering the lantern to shine on the ground ahead of them and tucking George's trembling arm neatly against his side as before. "Now, where is that Whiskers?" For once, George showed very little concern for her pet. But how could she? It was an almost overwhelming effort just to put one foot in front of the other. Perhaps a moonlit walk with an unattached, attractive young man—though he was only a friend—was indeed as unwise as the dictates of her conscience had suggested!

CHAPTER SEVEN

"PRINNY HAS HIS OWN in Brighton, you know, not more than a few yards from the royal tent," the viscount informed the group as they stood observing Mrs. Stone's bathing machine. "It is most ostentatiously decorated, not only with the royal arms, but with a pastoral scene by none other than the great John Constable himself!"

Three days had passed since Isabella had spoiled George's chances of a socially acceptable sea bath (unlike the one George had had the misfortune to encounter), and it was Lord Sarre who reintroduced the idea, delicately avoiding any reference to earlier conversations on the subject. Thus his lordship, George, Jane, Micah and a most reluctant Isabella had walked out on a fine, cloudless morning to patronize the bathing machines.

As it happened, Mrs. Ford had given up her duties as a "dipper" for a while. The door of her machine was firmly locked against intruders and the entire equipage dragged up onto high ground by her horse. It seemed her crutch had been inexorably claimed by a grasping sea wave and was probably, by now, washed up on the shores of Ireland.

Only the frequently bosky Mrs. Stone was left to patronize, and when Jane vocalized her concern over Mrs. Stone's ability to oversee the immersion and security of their guests, Tony obligingly offered to be nearby for assistance if necessary. When Jane, her eyes brimming with laughter, expressed her opinion that Tony was "queer in the attic if he supposed that rational women would allow themselves to be gaped at by the profligate likes of him while they frolicked in the sea!" and smote him soundly with her reticule, Tony tried to explain. Indeed, he'd had no intention of staying at the shore where he could see the ladies bathing, but meant to stand at some distance, only close enough to hear if any one of them required lifesaving measures to be initiated on their behalf. Finally the ladies were convinced that he and Micah had best postpone their own trip to Mr. Wheatley's bathing machine farther down the beach and remain nearby.

"It doesn't look as though anyone is here," said Isabella hopefully.

"Or Mrs. Stone is in her cups!" suggested Jane. "In that case, we'd better not bathe!"

The place did indeed appear deserted. The horse was put to the harness, certainly, but for what purpose George could not perceive since the beach was quite empty except for their small group.

"It is cruel to keep this poor beast out in the sun if no one is using the machine!" said George, walking nearer to rub the sway-backed hack's forelock and croon condolences into its ears, which were twitching lethargically against the incessant assault of a swarm of flies.

Suddenly the door swung open and Mrs. Stone appeared, her very large form entirely filling the opening.

"Good God!" ejaculated Micah beneath his breath.

But Jane, used to Mrs. Stone's formidable appearance, and perceiving that she was un-inebriated at present, stepped forward. "How do you do, Mrs. Stone? I've brought some of our guests to bathe in the sea! Are you open for business?"

"Always open for business, dearie," stated Mrs. Stone, fixing her bloodshot eyes on each of them in turn, and bringing the goose bumps up on George's arms. "Can't afford to be out o' business, no 'ow. Naw enough business to keep me 'ead above water as it is!"

George fervently hoped that Mrs. Stone was at least capable of keeping her bathers' heads above water.

"But I dawn't cater to gentlemen," she said, her fierce gaze boring into Lord Sarre and Micah. "This 'ere's a respectable business!"

"Good God!" Micah repeated, horrified at the very idea of relinquishing himself and his clothes to the likes of such a ham-handed woman!

"Mrs. Stone," said the viscount, his sense of the ridiculous considerably gratified by this giantess, shrouded in a black smock, her head wrapped up in a Paisley scarf with a wide-brimmed sort of sun-hat pushed low onto her broad forehead. "We've only escorted the ladies here. We intend to remove ourselves to another location as soon as they're ready to enter your machine."

"Then be off," she grunted. "They're comin' now."

Isabella had been standing stock-still ever since Mrs. Stone's appearance at the door. Her face was white and transfixed with dread. Now that she was being beckoned to ascend the short ladder to the door of the machine, she grasped the arm nearest to her and seemed incapable of letting go. The arm she fell upon happened to be Micah's. Nothing could have surprised him more and he commenced upon a series of blinks unequalled by any past performance George could remember.

"Isabella," he stammered. "What . . . What is it?"

"She is not quite the thing, you know," she whispered in a quavering voice, her dark eyes grown enormous as they continued to stare at Mrs. Stone.

To see Isabella's usual haughty demeanour reduced to such a childlike vulnerability took them all by surprise. While Mrs. Stone stood in offended silence, George tried to allay Isabella's fears by representing to her how very experienced Mrs. Stone was in her long career as a dipper, even though her own misgivings were considerably increased by that large madam's brusque manner.

"Mrs. Stone, give us a moment, please," said Jane, perceiving that Isabella's fingernails were still firmly impaled in the fabric of Micah's favourite powder-blue coat. Mrs. Stone snorted and retreated into the close confines of her bathing machine.

As George continued to entreat Isabella to be brave and described to her with enthusiasm the great good fun they'd have, Lord Sarre listened and watched and finally concluded that Isabella wasn't being the least influenced by these endeavours. And having suspected from the first that Isabella's delight in sea-bathing had been feigned to please him, said, "Perhaps Miss Lacy would prefer to return to the house?"

Isabella mutely nodded her favour of such a plan.

"Ah, then," continued the viscount, in a perfectly sober voice but with his green eyes dancing a jig, "as a most willing escort, I'd offer my arm, but it seems you already have one!"

Isabella's face took on a horrified aspect as she gradually realized upon whom she'd been leaning for comfort. Releasing Micah's arm with such rapidity that it might have been a viper, she seemed to shake off the momentary weakness she'd been indulging and lifted her chin to its usual lofty heights, saying, "No! I don't want to return to the house. I was only a little discomposed by the vulgarity of Mrs. Stone! Mrs. Gunn, in Brighton you know, is a great deal more refined. But then I should not have expected anything above the most ordinary in *Bleadon!*"

Such ill-mannered expressions were unanswerable. The viscount threw George and Jane a commiserative look and bade them goodbye for the present. Then, dragging a still-astonished Micah with him, he repaired to a sandy hill several yards away.

As the ladies entered the bathing machine, George was struck by how very hot it was inside. She wondered that Mrs. Stone could sit in it without succumbing to a swoon. However, when that lady ordered them to strip themselves of all their clothing, George quite forgot modesty and obeyed her immediately. She could not wait to step outside the door and immerse herself in the cool waters.

Once the ladies were unclothed and their garments hung on hooks that lined the wall, the proprietor gave them each a bathing gown not unlike the one she wore herself—black, shapeless sacks with sleeves that flared to just below the elbows and hems that skimmed the floor. In fact, since George was so short, a portion of her gown actually lay on the floor and she had to lift it lest she tangle her feet in its voluminous folds.

"It's the smallest size I have, dearie," Mrs. Stone informed her unsympathetically. "Now loosen your hair—there, that's right! If you don't take the pretty pins and combs out, the sea will!" she warned them.

Finally they'd finished their preparations and were to be allowed outside the dark, minuscule hut and into the sunshine as soon as the horse had backed the machine into the shallow depths of the sea. The door was opened at last and the ladder let down so that they could descend into the water.

Jane led the way and George eagerly followed. Isabella, silent throughout the entire disrobing process, was nudged forwards by Mrs. Stone until she had been fairly forced to go out whether she truly wanted to or not. But as stubborn as she was fearful, Isabella seemed to have decided to do the deed for the approbation of the viscount, despite her utter distaste for sharing a bath with an unknown quantity and variety of marine life. They waded out until the water lapped as high as George's chest.

Mrs. Stone stood in the water with them and issued instructions and warnings in a constant flow, one moment righting Isabella whose feet had come out from under her, and the next moment admonishing George to stop thrashing about in the water or she would certainly have to punish her for overstepping what was "seemly" in the water and send her back into the bathing machine forthwith.

George was having a wonderful time! Despite the surf's persistent tugging at the heavy gown she was compelled to wear, the surge and dip of the tingly water against her skin was wonderfully refreshing. She wanted to splash and laugh and dive beneath the surface; and she did until Mrs. Stone again called her severely to order. Jane behaved more circumspectly, only bouncing about gently and smiling. After a time, even Isabella relaxed, smiling despite herself and leaning back in the water to let her long strands of hair float in a fanned shape about her head. To George, in that particular position, she looked like Medusa. But rather than spoil Isabella's improved mood by suggesting the dubious comparison, George laughed out loud and imitated the pose, completely untroubled that her much shorter hair could not hope to look in any way similar.

THE VISCOUNT AND MICAH had been sitting for what seemed like an age in the hot sun before they saw Mrs. Stone guiding the horse into the water. As she moved around to the front of the bathing machine, the huge wheels of which were now immersed in two feet of water, Lord Sarre strained to see if the ladies were observable at all from such a distant vantage point. Three differently coloured heads emerged, all of the ladies wearing black smocks like Mrs. Stone's, looking for all the world like a covey of nuns on holiday. But— damn!—he wished he could see George's face just now! How she must be enjoying herself!

"Deuced fine-looking woman, Isabella! Shame she's so high in the instep! Didn't used to be!" the viscount heard Micah muttering. When he turned to ask his friend why Isabella's imperfections were suddenly such a source of vexation, he found him peering through a pair of opera glasses.

"Good gad, Micah! What are you doing?" he demanded, amused and appalled at the same time.

"Why, what do you think I'm doing? Looking at the girls! All fine-looking, of course, but Isabella has it all over the others when it comes to being well-endowed, if you catch my meaning! What a strapper!"

"Has it never occurred to you, Micah," the viscount enquired in a tone of wry exasperation, "that what you're doing is a serious breach of propriety and that any one of those fine-looking young women would cut your acquaintance—not to mention your throat!—if they happened to discover you ogling them in such a way?"

"Won't know anything about it 'less you tell them, Tony," replied Micah, completely unperturbed. "George is flying high! Look at her splash and jump!"

The viscount looked—very hard indeed!—but all he could see was the reflection of the sun off her golden head and that small glossy orb bouncing up and down like a buoy. It was maddeningly frustrating, but to stoop to Micah's standard and employ a pair of opera glasses to play Peeping Tom was out of the question!

Frustration was fast becoming the order of the day in Lord Sarre's life. Ever since he'd lured George out of her bedchamber and onto the beach for a moonlit walk, she'd been more skittish than ever. Always happy to see him, she'd smile radiantly whenever he entered a room. Then, as if she'd thought better of it, she'd stifle her smiles and limit her conversation and manners to all that was most proper and demure. If he only knew precisely what she thought of him, he'd know how to go on!

"Jane is the most sedate," Micah was saying now, "but I expect she is used to the sea. Handsome girl,

Jane. Isabella seems uncommonly fond of floating on her back.... Daresay floating is no problem for such a buxom lass as she!''

''And *gloating* is no problem for you, Micah,'' observed the viscount testily. He was annoyed at Micah for having the gall to pocket a pair of opera glasses for the express purpose of spying on the ladies, and even more annoyed with himself for the overwhelming urge he had to snatch them away and take a look himself! He didn't have the smallest desire to observe Isabella's charms. *They* were commonplace enough. But the image of George as she'd looked the other day, all wet and winsome, gnawed at his self-control unceasingly. Ah, to see her in just that way again!

''Now George is laughing and throwing her head back in the water like Isabella! What a plucky bit of a girl she is! Reminds me of the time we took a dip in Bromley's pond....''

Lord Sarre turned on his friend and glared quite fiercely. Sensing that the viscount's displeasure had been aroused, Micah quickly explained. ''Only eight years old, Tony! Needn't worry! Isabella was there, too! B'sides, always been on the up-and-up with George! She'd have given me pepper otherwise, just as she did t'other day.''

Lord Sarre acknowledged the truth of it and returned his brooding gaze to the sea.

''Nymphish-looking, George is,'' Micah's commentary continued. ''With that gamine face and pixie hair she's a sea nymph if ever I saw one!''

Goaded beyond human endurance, Lord Sarre snatched away the opera glasses, affixed them to his face and searched for the elf who had stolen his heart and every shred of self-respect he'd owned before this fateful moment.

Finding her at last within the scope of his lenses, he had only a moment to feast his eyes before being rudely interrupted by the most unexpected source: his grandmother.

"Anthony Charles Braithwaite, you scapegrace! For shame!"

Having been privileged to hear these words on only one or two memorable occasions since he'd reached his majority, Lord Sarre was taken back quite forcefully to his childhood. Suddenly he was six years old again, his pockets full of bugs and worms, his Sunday shoes muddied beyond repair and his grubby hands hidden behind his back. And Grandmother Braithwaite was delivering a thundering scold.

Turning slowly, the tell-tale opera glasses still clutched in one hand, he observed the dreaded presence of his diminutive grandmother on the arm of his brother John. She'd twisted her lips into such a comical attempt at disapproval, Lord Sarre was hard pressed not to laugh, especially since John seemed to be enjoying the encounter more than he ought!

"How do you do, Grandmother?" the viscount said, standing up and vigorously shaking the opera glasses behind his back as he bent over to kiss her withered cheek. Micah finally understood that his friend was endeavouring to rid himself of the glasses, and he took them and tucked them away in his pocket. "And John! You're looking fit as a fiddle, as they say!" he announced blandly, extending the hand which had been so recently polluted by the tool of the crime, and trying hard to appear unaware that he'd transgressed any rules of conduct.

As they shook hands, John gleefully observed, "Never thought I'd see Lord Sarre, the unchallenged nonpareil, stoop to such dubious shenanigans! Much obliged, Tony! You've made my day!"

"I live to amuse you, brother," returned the viscount with a rueful grin. "But if I've ever done anything which you regard as a special favour, on the strength of that one noble deed I implore you to forget what you've just seen. I'm heartily ashamed of myself and am unable to offer any explanation at present. But I assure you—"

"Stuff and nonsense!" Lady Sarre broke in, unclamping her mouth from its former indignant pose to voice her opinion. "Needn't try to wrap it up in clean linen! Saw what you were doing! No explanation necessary! If you weren't such a tall, large fellow, I'd take you over my knee, just as I used to do, and thrash the living daylights out of you!"

"Grandmother," interrupted his lordship, hoping fervently to nip the tirade of righteous indignation in the bud by introducing Micah to her notice, "It seems I've quite forgotten my manners—"

"And your morals!" she snapped.

"Those, I fear, were lost an age ago," Lord Sarre responded good-humouredly. "This is Micah Shelby. You may remember meeting him at Aldsworth once or twice."

"Of course I remember him! Haven't lost my wits yet, you young rapscallion!" she retorted, punctuating her point by jabbing the viscount in the ribs with her parasol.

"Charmed to see you again, my lady," Micah ventured to say with a polite little bow, all the while eyeing the dowager's parasol with misgiving.

"Don't humbug me, Mr. Shelby," she told him with a severe look. "You aren't the least bit charmed to see me! And I'm sure you won't mind if I confess that I'm not the least pleased to see you, either! And if you hope ever to find favour with me, young man, you'll have to discontinue that confounded habit you have of blinking! Drives a person to distraction!"

Thrown into utter confusion by this forthright speech, Micah was unable to respond in any way. Conscious that he felt the need to blink with an increased urgency since the dowager had brought it to his attention, he endeavoured to refrain and was rewarded for his success by being told that if he persisted in staring in that rude, owlish way she would not be held accountable for her actions! Micah decided that he'd best remove himself from the vicinity of the lady's parasol and look at his shoes.

Taking his grandmother's other arm and mercifully allowing Micah to walk behind, Lord Sarre said,

"To what do we owe this visit, Grandmother? Knowing your distaste for coaching inns and the tedium of travel, I'd had no hope of seeing you in Bleadon when I wrote and asked John to join me here."

"Bored, Anthony! Bored beyond bearing! I've a lively mind and I'm tired of confining my activities to bullying the poor and depressed of the neighbourhood into prosperity and happiness!"

The viscount exchanged a speaking look with John. They both knew this meant that Lady Sarre was itching to meddle. Looking down at the tiny, aged woman at his side, he was painfully aware to what extent she was capable of meddling. She always meant well, of course, her heart being quite large, but her opinions were strong and forcibly shared with all the chosen victims of her good intentions. Even now, as her green eyes restlessly combed the beach, they snapped with energy and speculation.

Lord Sarre sighed and hoped that his grandmother would not complicate a situation that was fast becoming a tangle only the most delicate machinations could unravel. As they walked, he began to question John as to the general conditions at Aldsworth. While John responded to these questions, Lord Sarre looked him over closely. Though John was shorter and slighter than he, he'd been a wiry lad, able to out-run, out-box and out-smart his contemporaries with regularity. It had seemed the natural choice for such an active, vital youth to choose the army as his profession, and his father had duly bought him a captaincy in the

Ninth Hussar Guards. A bruiser on horseback and a determined patriot for England, he'd soon made a dashing name for himself and filled his father's remaining days on earth with paternal pride.

It was while John was in Brussels that Lord Sarre died. The viscount had often blessed the timing of their father's release from a lingering illness, because it would have caused the old gentleman no end of suffering if he'd witnessed the pain endured by John at the loss of his leg. But for John the death of his beloved father was a severe blow. Such a double calamity in his heretofore sparkling existence sent him into a deep depression. And being bedridden for such an extended period, he was denied the one thing that might have eased his mental anguish—activity. To have been so vital and busy before and so immersed in his budding career, and then to be suddenly denied everything, was too much to bear.

A year had passed and John seemed to have recovered, or so, at least, it appeared to those who did not know him as well as his brother. He had taught himself to walk with admirable grace on his peg-leg and had taken an active part in managing the estate at Aldsworth. Lord Sarre could have easily managed it himself, of course, but he knew that John needed something to do. But overseeing his brother's estate would not keep a man with John's mental and physical powers happy for long.

Thinner even than the last time Lord Sarre had seen him, John's face was drawn and pale. The viscount was convinced that his brother was fretting himself sick and hiding it behind a façade of pleasantries. He was still suffering, but he suffered privately, confiding in no one. But Lord Sarre felt he knew John's innermost thoughts. He imagined just how wretched *he* would feel in the same situation: how purposeless, how un-manned and how unworthy of someone who could charm his days and nights with happiness... But enough was enough! He hoped with fervour that his plan would prove the antidote to John's self-loathing. John deserved to be happy, and by God he would be if Tony had anything to say about it!

"Tony, a word please," said Micah, tapping him on the shoulder. The viscount excused himself and disengaged his arm from his grandmother's, stepping a few paces away to discover what Micah wanted. "Think we ought not to wander too far afield, Tony," Micah suggested, jerking his head in the direction of the bathing machine. "Told the ladies we'd be close by in case they needed us, y'know."

"I don't think they shall be needing us since Mrs. Stone appears to be sober today. But I agree that we should wait for them or they'll wonder what became of us." His brows knitted thoughtfully. "We have quite an evening ahead of us, Micah." And with this enigmatic statement Lord Sarre rejoined his relatives and guided them back to the beach.

GLOWING FROM THE EXERCISE and sun (not to mention the brisk rubbing down Mrs. Stone had given them after their bath) the girls were in fine fettle when they trod up the beach to meet the others. They'd wrung their hair as dry as they could, towelled it, then twisted it into knots at their crowns, plopping a bonnet over their make-do coiffures until their abigails could do better. At first Jane held back when she observed the additions to their party, but after a slight hesitation and a deep blush, she seemed to lift her chin and step purposefully forward, as if meeting her fate.

"Miss Lacy, Miss Georgiana," said the viscount as they reached him. "Allow me to introduce my grandmother, Lady Sarre, and my brother, Captain John Braithwaite."

George was impressed with the captain, finding him very good-looking, despite his slightly gaunt appearance, with a military polish to his country gentleman's dress which set off his narrow hips and nicely turned leg to advantage. He smiled and said all that was proper, but George sensed a carefully controlled agitation emanating from the captain. Then he turned to address Jane.

"Jane. How are you?" he said, taking her hand but not kissing it as Tony had done. His eyes flickered over her, but strayed to a point somewhere off in the distance.

"Tolerable," she replied quietly. She evidently did not feel the same need as the captain to avert her eyes. She looked him over thoroughly and then fixed her gaze upon his face until he returned her searching look with a rather pained one. But George was not granted more opportunity to observe the two, because Lady Sarre had been ignored long enough.

"And how was your bath, girls?" she demanded to know once they'd each duly curtsied and Jane had kissed her grandmother's cheek. "Do not say 'tolerable' in that insipid way as Jane just did. You're blooming! There's nothing as healthy and invigorating as a sea bath, I say!"

"She also endorses the heathenish fashion of rolling oneself in the snow to restore circulation," said the viscount dryly. "So please do not change all your habits on the strength of my grandmother's recommendations. Her constitution is so hearty that I don't doubt she'll outlive us all!"

"I enjoyed the bath prodigiously!" announced Isabella, a note of wonder creeping into her voice as if she did not quite believe it.

"Knew you'd enjoy it, Isa—Miss Lacy!" Micah ventured to say. "Used to like Squire Bromley's pond, as I recall!"

Isabella looked startled, as if she'd quite forgotten the squire's pond and the times they'd spent there as children, and she gazed at Micah for a moment with something like affection in her eyes. Then, jerking her eyes resolutely away, she replied in a quelling tone, "Yes, but the sea can hardly be compared with Bromley's pond, Micah! Pray, don't be absurd!"

Striving to divert everyone's attention from Micah's flushing face, George said, "I think we all had an enjoyable time, but Mrs. Stone disapproved of us.

We were not sedate enough to please her! She said we splashed too much and were sad romps!"

"Yes, I know," said Micah. Then, when all eyes were turned to him, he amended, "I mean—that is to say—knew you'd give old Stoney a run for her money. You girls are plucky, deuced plucky!"

Perceiving that they'd received a compliment of some sort, the ladies were satisfied to let the subject drop, while Micah sighed with relief.

"How do you find Bleadon after such an absence?" Jane asked the captain in a constrained voice.

"Much the same," he replied thoughtfully, a look of nostalgia seeming to glaze his green Braithwaite eyes as they roamed over the undulating sands. "It has been a long time," he mused, lifting his head to watch a gull sweep overhead.

"A year last month," supplied Jane.

The captain was arrested by the quiet emphasis of Jane's words. For the first time he really looked at her, and the two pairs of eyes locked for an endless moment. George began to feel awkward and wished someone would speak. Finally the captain said, "You are precise, Jane."

"Only sometimes," she said, smiling faintly.

"Isn't it time for nuncheon?" said the Dowager Viscountess. "Let's return to the house straightaway! I'm famished and I know you girls must be also! I met your mother," she informed George, taking her arm and steering her towards the hill. "You aren't at all alike, you know. Why, I quite like *you!* Take after your father, I daresay.''

''Only in looks,'' George said, her voice trembling with suppressed laughter.

''Then you are an original, Miss Georgiana,'' Lady Sarre pronounced, making George wonder at so decided an opinion after an acquaintance of five minutes.

''Come along!'' called the dowager over her shoulder, and the others meekly fell into line behind her.

CHAPTER EIGHT

PERKINS HAD GROWN USED to dressing Miss Georgiana Lacy for dinner and had even come to prefer her to her elder sister. The younger Miss Lacy was never rude and did not waste precious time primping and preening before the mirror between putting on each piece of clothing or each stroke of the hairbrush.

Tonight, with the elegantly dressed Dowager Viscountess Sarre and the pale, but interesting, Captain Braithwaite to impress, Perkins fussed over George until that young lady emerged, a pastel vision of beguiling youth. The diaphanous peach overskirt of Norwich lace draped charmingly over the sleek underskirt of ivory silk. George's small breasts peeked out, pristinely white, above the lace ruching of her bodice, and the delicate colour produced by her fifteen-minute sojourn in the sea bloomed on her cheeks.

"This is an interesting style, Perkins," George was saying as she tilted her head from side to side to observe the finished creation. "What do you call it?"

"It hasn't a name, Miss Georgiana. I just decided to make the best use of your natural curls. Since they seem determined to riot, we shall let them!"

Indeed, thought George, except for the French twist in the back and the band of silk peach-colored orchids placed high on her crown, her hair *was* a riot of curls!

For some time now, George had been aware of subtle changes occurring in her attitude. She did not mind looking pretty; in fact she rather liked it! But a thorough investigation of the reasons for this change she tried hard to avoid. As she was not stupid, thoughts of a romantic attachment for the viscount *had* entered her mind. In truth, such thoughts had claimed her attention a night or two to the exclusion of sleep! But since she was sure he intended to marry either his cousin Jane, or her own sister Isabella, speculations about his feelings towards her seemed pointless.

Tony was a very kind friend; what more could she ask for? And as a wife, she wouldn't do at all! Probably if he were to look at her for wifely qualities, he'd find much to criticize. She could not bear that! And who's to say she would like *him* as a husband? She'd certainly never enjoyed the romantic overtures of any other of her acquaintance. It was best to remain friends, after all, she concluded. But even as friends she couldn't justify another moonlit walk on the beach. Such activities were capable of putting strange ideas into even the most sensible young woman's head.

Thanking Perkins very prettily for her exertions, George dismissed the abigail and glanced at the clock on the mantel-shelf. There was still half an hour 'til dinner would be announced, and she was reluctant to enter the drawing-room without knowing whom she was likely to find there. Lady Sarre frightened her a little with her sharp eyes and unpredictable tongue, despite that lady's unaccountable partiality for her, and Captain Braithwaite so engaged her tender sympathies and respect she found it difficult to speak to him without alluding to his bravery at Waterloo. Whether that would be a welcome subject, she doubted very much. He seemed unhappy to her, beneath his easy, friendly manners, and she hoped Tony's plans to help his brother (whatever they were) would be successful.

As for Jane, George could hardly recognize the moody, preoccupied young woman Jane now was as the confiding, friendly person she'd met on their arrival. She hadn't even had a chance to ask Jane why she'd kept her from mentioning Tony's walk with that man on the cliff. Something else that puzzled George was the palpable tension that quivered between Jane and the captain. If anyone else noticed it, they didn't let on. Perhaps the two of them had had a quarrel in the past which had kept him away from Bleadon. She determined to ask Tony about it.

Having shared a rare, pleasant experience with her sister that morning, similar to times they'd enjoyed as children, George decided to visit Isabella's bedchamber and perhaps engage in a little friendly chatter before dinner. Realizing that she was probably being more optimistic than experience would encourage, she nonetheless set off for that part of the house with a light step.

As she reached the door to Isabella's room, Perkins was just coming out. The abigail smiled and stepped aside to allow George to pass through, closing the door quietly behind her. George had taken only one step into the room when she was arrested by the sound of her mother's querulous voice, coming from behind the screen Perkins had placed around Isabella's dressing-table to ward off the late-afternoon sun glaring in through the westwardly facing windows.

"Lord Sarre is taking too long, Isabella! You have to do it, my angel! When the game goes on and on and the players grow fatigued and bored!"

George was fully aware that her mother and Isabella thought they were alone and she was quite shamelessly eavesdropping, but it sounded as though they were plotting against Tony in some way and her hackles rose. Pressing herself into the shadows of the huge wardrobe, which barely contained Isabella's prodigious supply of gowns, she listened.

"But Mama, how do I go about such a task?" cried Isabella so petulantly that George could easily imagine the pout on her face. "I've never been compromised before! I don't know how the thing's to be done!"

George drew in her breath, shocked by the vulgar depths to which her mother's ambitions for Isabella had sunk her.

"I've not worked out the details, but I daresay it may be contrived easily enough. The fact that his grandmother is here and is such a stickler for propriety should help to bring the viscount up to scratch when the two of you are discovered in a compromising pose of some sort."

"What a tiresome business this is!" Isabella whined. "I shall be heartily glad to be married if I can then do as I please! But must it be the viscount? I begin to wonder if he's what I would wish for in a husband!"

"Isabella!" snapped her mother, aghast at such a traitorous sentiment to all she held near and dear. "He is rich, he is titled, he is impeccably positioned in the ton! What more could you possibly want? Crested carriages, jewellery, your very own house in Town for the Season, dinners with the aristocracy... Only think of it, Isabella! And *I* shall come to visit you, my angel!"

"Well, I suppose he'll do as well as the next nobleman that may come along," was her not very enthusiastic reply.

"And what if you bungle this chance, Isabella, and no other nobleman *should* come along?" taunted her mother. "You're twenty years old, and despite your beauty may find yourself on the shelf if you do not take advantage of the present situation. The viscount has already proven he is quite susceptible to your charms by forgiving you for that unfortunate slip of the tongue the other morning." She stopped and then continued momentarily in a considering voice. "Hmm...if he found himself quite alone with you..."

"So far, that has never occurred, though I haven't guarded against it in the least!" admitted Isabella sulkily.

"...with no apparent danger of interruption..."

"And how do you propose to accomplish that, madam?" enquired Isabella sceptically.

"Leave it to me, child! When the propitious moment arrives, I'll know just what to do! It's a shame the viscount doesn't drink excessively. If he were foxed the deed might be done in a trice! But you must promise me to co-operate in every detail!" When Isabella did not immediately answer, her mother raised her voice. "Isabella?"

"Oh, very well! What do you wish me to do?"

George tensed and strained her ears to hear every detail of her mother's nefarious scheme, but was disappointed when none was forthcoming. "I must think on it a little longer, Isabella, but now we'd best go down to the drawing-room. Do be civil to his crippled brother! All doubt must be removed from the viscount's mind in that direction...."

A rustling of skirts declared that the ladies were on the point of arising and, after a last look in the mirror, would soon be walking to the door. Swiftly and noiselessly, George returned to the door, opened it and shut it, taking care that her supposed entry into the room was as noisy as possible.

"Good evening, Mama, Isabella!" she chirped. "Thought I'd step in to see how you fare after your sea bath this morning, sister!"

"It was fatiguing!" stated Isabella dampeningly, her down-turned mouth evidence of her sulky mood. "If not for my very short nap after nuncheon—lasted a mere two hours before Perkins woke me with her confounded clattering about the room—I should be fagged to death! I hope you do not suppose I enjoyed myself!"

"I do own I'm surprised," said George, her eyebrows lifting. "I thought you were having a prodigious good time if smiling and laughing are to be considered any indication of one's enjoyment! And you did tell the viscount you enjoyed yourself," she challenged, a militant gleam in her eyes.

"As I've said on numerous occasions before, George," Isabella deigned to reply with civil indifference. "You know nothing about gentlemen or the art of attracting them, so please refrain from comments, if you please!"

"Indeed!" agreed her mother, sweeping past her younger daughter to the door. "Now please, girls," she admonished with her hand on the knob, "do behave yourselves this evening."

George silently followed them out the door and down the hall, all the while determining how best to dupe their vulgar designs upon Tony's title and fortune. After all, as a friend, it was her duty to save him.

IT HAD STARTED RAINING shortly after nuncheon, but it was such an inconsequential drizzle, George expected the sky to have cleared by dinner. However, it had not. Now the rain pelted the windows, and the small trees surrounding the house bowed in humble tribute to the force of the wind coming off the turbulent sea.

Coincidentally, the admiral's toe had worsened as well. It was now so swollen no shoe or boot could accommodate its size and Admiral Braithwaite was forced to greet his guests in stockings. Of course he could wear one boot, but it seemed too ridiculous a compromise and would, at any rate, render him lopsided. His military bearing would suffer in such a case, but in his stockings at least he could stand as straight as ever.

When George entered the drawing-room with her mother and Isabella, the only other occupants were the admiral and Lady Sarre. Sitting next to her son on the sofa, the dowager was offering opinions on the state of his big toe. She did not credit his discomfort to the weather, but to port. According to the dowager, he drank too much of it!

"Madam, have you noticed the rain?" he asked her with asperity, grimacing as he shifted his foot from a low footstool to the floor.

"Yes indeed, and the wind is blowing rather strongly, too!" she answered cheerfully. "But you'll never convince me, Jacob, that your gout and the weather are in any way connected!"

The admiral was forming a fitting rebuttal for his faithless parent, but perceiving his guests entering the room he stood up to greet them.

"Oh sit down, Admiral!" cried George. "You needn't stand on points with us! I know your toe is paining you!"

The admiral dutifully bowed over each lady's hand and was about to thank George for her concern when the dowager interrupted.

"Miss Georgiana is as sweet as she is pretty, but I must disagree with her! A gentleman should always rise when a lady enters the room. A little pain is good for the character!"

Since neither Mrs. Lacy or Isabella had much affection for pain they rolled their eyes at each other and kept silent.

"Sit here, Miss Georgiana," the dowager commanded, patting the empty space next to her on the sofa. "Sit by me! I like you!"

"But 'tis the admiral's seat," she demurred.

"Take it and welcome," growled the admiral, limping his way to a chair at some distance from his mother.

George had no choice but to sit. She was aware that such a great lady's notice ought to be appreciated. However, she did not enjoy the attention Lady Sarre had been paying her since they'd first met on the beach, because it only drew censorious glares from her mother and sister.

Presently the rest of the party trickled in, one by one. At dinner everyone behaved just as they had at nuncheon. Isabella flirted; her mother simpered and nodded approvingly; Micah joked and blinked; Jane was silent, blushing and withdrawn; the admiral predicted a hurricane and winced whenever he moved his foot; the dowager interrupted everyone's conversations with unsolicited opinions; and Captain Braithwaite smiled and spoke pleasantly whenever he was addressed.

As for the viscount, he was as charming as ever, spinning the silken thread of congeniality and tact which saved the group from many a pitfall of bad taste or contention. And despite such a time-consuming drain on his abilities, though he sat too far away for conversation, Lord Sarre managed to smile at George on several occasions. Once, when his eyes seemed to take in each part of her, moving with purpose from her face to her hair, then down to the puffed lace of her sleeves and over to the white swell of her décolletage, George dropped her eyes and unconsciously lifted her hand to rest it protectively against her chest. When she looked again, Tony was talking to his uncle and she supposed she must have imagined that strange look in his eyes.

The rest of the evening flew by in a whirl of conversation, music and cards. All the while, the formal civilization of the drawing-room made a striking contrast to the wild, unfettered raging of the storm. George was a little uneasy, but was ashamed to admit it since no one except the admiral seemed to notice or care what was progressing outside.

She cudgeled her brain for a solution to Tony's problem and was forced to admit that he'd have to be warned about her mother's plan to trap him into marriage with Isabella. She dare not tell him herself—she was too ashamed of her family to be able to face him!—but Micah would do it for her. Determined to employ Micah's assistance as soon as possible, she waited patiently, but no opportunity arose. Whenever she contrived to catch Micah alone, he wandered away to stand and gape at her sister! George found his behaviour frustrating (not to mention odd) but she was used to men gaping at Isabella, whether they liked her sister or not.

Presently it was time to retire to the bedchambers and George was forced to keep her secret until the morning. A languid comment or two was exchanged about how depressing to the spirit inclement weather was and how they hoped it would be calmer tomorrow, but that seemed to be the extent to which the others were concerned.

When George reached her bedchamber she drew the drapes from across the French doors and peered out into the night. A driving rain pounded against the glass and a strong wind penetrated even the smallest cracks around the door frame, enveloping George in a swirl of cold air. Only faraway rumbles of thunder had punctuated the sounds of the storm before—the persistent pummelling of rain on the roof and the gust and whistle of the wind—but now lightning flashed and a clap of thunder fairly shook George out of her shoes.

Suddenly she remembered Whiskers. Cook probably had him snugly tucked into the covers at the bottom of her bed, but George had to be sure. Taking a candle with her, she left the room and walked down the back stairway to the kitchen. All was dark and quiet there; even the embers of the cooking fire had been completely extinguished by the draft coming down the chimney.

She was loath to wake the good-natured servant, but walked through the kitchen and down a narrow hall to the room she knew belonged to the cook. At least, she told herself, it was not as if she were waking someone truly unpleasant like her mother. She knocked on the door and was rewarded by the sound of a drowsy "Who is it?" and a lusty bark.

"Never mind, Mrs. Higgens," she called out in a loud whisper. "I only wanted to look in on Whiskers. He's afraid of the thunder, you know! Since he's with you, I'll not worry. Or do you wish me to take him?"

Mrs. Higgens came to the door dressed in a voluminous flannel nightgown and mob cap. She was holding Whiskers in her beefy arms and he seemed to be quite content to remain where he was.

"All's right and tight here, miss," said Mrs. Higgens. "I saw the little rat was afeared of the storm and I brung him to bed with me."

There was another loud clap of thunder and Whiskers hid his head under one of Mrs. Higgen's large breasts.

"Ha!" laughed the servant. "I hoped they'd be good for somethin' after my poor old Tom turned up his toes!"

George was a little embarrassed by the servant's bawdy humour, but was grateful nonetheless for her kindness to Whiskers. She thanked Mrs. Higgens and gave her dog a parting pat. When the door was again shut, she walked slowly down the hall to the kitchen, feeling rather abandoned and lonely. Maybe she was as frightened of the storm as Whiskers! At any rate, she could do with a little company right now.

She passed through the kitchen and was about to ascend the stairs to the gallery leading to her room when she heard voices somewhere nearby. Since she was still fully clothed, she thought she might as well investigate and possibly dredge up a little company. She opened a door and found herself in another back hallway. There was a closed door, and from her limited knowledge of the house she thought it might be the back entrance to the library. Now the voices were distinguishable. It was Tony and the captain.

She was about to withdraw reluctantly, since she supposed they had brotherly things to discuss which her presence would hinder, when she heard the captain say, "Tony, out with it! You know that Bleadon is the last place on God's green earth I want to be, so you'd damned well better have a good explanation for sending for me in such a high-handed manner!''

George stepped closer to the door and leaned into the embrasure. It was humiliating to find herself for the second time in one day willingly eavesdropping!

"It wasn't meant to be an order, John. If that is how you perceived it, I beg your pardon," said the viscount placatingly.

"You said it was imperative that I come. You said you had a matter to discuss with me that was secret in nature, but I was not to reveal the urgency of your summons! Good God, Tony, I half-expected to find you in some horrid tangle! Debts, duels or a wronged woman on a murderous quest ranged through my imagination vividly! Instead I find you leering at three women bathing in the sea—one of them our cousin!— through a pair of opera glasses!"

George nearly dropped her candle at this revelation, but gripped the handle rather more firmly and was now resolved to hear all!

"You always did have a healthy imagination, John. You must have been agitated when you received my letter, and that's why Grandmother decided to come with you. She cannot bear to be left out of anything!"

"I don't wish to talk about Grandmother's penchant for meddling, Tony! Again I say, out with it! But I warn you, if your summons was only a trick to get Jane and me together again...! I thought she was touring the Lake District or you can be assured I should not have come! If you only knew how wretched it makes me to be near her!''

John's voice broke and George's eyes misted with sympathetic tears. John was in love with Jane! Did she return his affection? George wondered. She had felt the tension between them. Was it a mutual attraction?

George heard several successive footsteps on the hardwood floor. She imagined that Tony was crossing the room to place a comforting hand on his brother's shoulder.

"You needn't be wretched, John. Jane still loves you! She told me so the very first day I was here. We were walking on the beach." So that was what they'd been talking about so earnestly! thought George. "I didn't bring it up. She did. I told her not to lose heart because..."

"Well, you shouldn't have encouraged her in the least!" John said bitterly. "She's in love with the man I *used* to be! Have you observed how silent and withdrawn she is now that she's seen this damned piece of wood!"

"She's silent, John, because she's feeling a great deal!"

"I don't want her pity!"

"It isn't pity. Damn it, man, will you listen to reason!" Now George could hear Tony pacing the floor.

"I'm going to bed," John said. "And tomorrow, if the roads are decent, I'm leaving! It was stupid of you to trick me into coming here. Jane deserves a complete husband, not some wrecked..."

"Sit down, John! I give you my word, I didn't bring you here to see Jane! I didn't even know she was here. I do have business to discuss with you. It was providence that brought Jane home early, and I saw no reason to mention it in my letter."

"You and providence can go to hell!" snarled the captain, obviously overwrought.

"Calm yourself, John, and listen to me. I've bought some land in Bleadon, quite a lot of it. You remember the down at the top of the hill?"

"Yes, what of it?"

"Remember when that fellow from Liverpool had decided to retire here and build the place into a fashionable resort?"

"More fool he! He hadn't the vision or the money for such a scheme!"

"Well, then I'm a worse fool, because I propose to do the very same thing. But *I* have money!"

"Why would you want to do such a thing, Tony?" asked the captain incredulously, seeming to forget his misery for a moment in his surprise. "You've enough to do. For such an enterprise to be a success someone would have to be here overseeing the building, and travelling back and forth to Bristol and Bath to talk it up amongst the nobs! You'd never be happy living in Bleadon so much of the year. You never cared for it as I do...."

There was a long pause. "Yes. As you do, John. You're the perfect candidate for such a project. And while I have the money, you, my dear brother, are the one endowed with vision!"

After another long pause, the captain said, "You're forcing me to make a very difficult decision, Tony. By God, I'd love such a task! It would be just the thing for me to do now that I'm denied the army. But Jane is here!"

"Yes," agreed his brother simply. "Jane is here!"

So much was clear to George now. The man on the cliff with Tony, Jane's behaviour, the viscount's need to keep things secret. He evidently did not want John to be forced into anything. He wanted to assemble and present a challenge to John and allow him to make a decision on his own. But Jane, at least, must have known. That was why she'd stopped her the other morning when she'd tried to question Tony about it at breakfast.

"Since I've at long last reduced you to silence, John," said the viscount amiably, "I've something to confide. It concerns Miss Georgiana Lacy...."

So shocked was George to hear her own name she dropped the candle. It clattered to the floor and she was sure it could be plainly heard on the other side of the door, despite the thundering storm. She stooped to pick it up and scurry away, but before the deed was done, the library door swung open. Especially awe-inspiring from such a low vantage point, the viscount towered above her. George's eyes travelled the length of him, from his stockinged feet (he had shed his boots), past the smooth pantaloons, stylish waistcoat and frothy neckcloth, and right up to his astonished green eyes.

"How do you come to be here, Miss Georgiana?" he asked her, the side of his mouth twitching rather oddly.

"I . . . I came to see about Whiskers," George stammered.

"Ah, I see!" he said, crossing his arms on his chest like a sultan, as his mouth broadened to a glinting smile such as a harem-keeper would save for his favourite concubine.

Appalled by the images this unlucky comparison had brought to mind, she blurted, "You know how he's frightened by the thunder, Tony! But . . . but Mrs. Higgens seems to be taking quite good care of him."

Now John stood at the door, too, just behind Tony. "How do you do, Miss Georgiana," said the captain politely, but George observed his mouth to be twitching as relentlessly as his brother's had.

"So glad to hear Whiskers is safe and warm," observed the viscount. "I had been thinking of him all night! But isn't Mrs. Higgens's room on the other side of the kitchen? Seems to me, George, you're quite lost. Shall I escort you to your room?"

"That isn't necessary," she assured him hastily. "To tell the truth, Tony, I had seen the door leading into this hallway and was compelled to see where it led. But

I'd only just arrived, you see, and then—so clumsy of me!—I dropped the candle!''

"Well, Miss Georgiana, I suppose I should not be surprised. With such a wondrous large curiosity as you profess to own, I can imagine what a temptation an obscure hallway on a dark, stormy night might be!''

Strongly suspecting that the viscount was roasting her, George's hackles rose. She was about to throw caution to the wind and ask him about the opera glasses, when John drew himself up suddenly, his face a mask of intense concentration.

"What is it, John?'' asked the viscount.

"I hear something.''

"What? How can you hear anything above this din?''

John cocked his head to the side. "Tony, I'm quite serious! It's as though someone were calling for help!'' They all stood absolutely still and listened. "Several people, men's voices actually!''

John walked swiftly to the library window which faced the sea. "Can't see a bloody thing through all this rain,'' he concluded at last and proceeded towards the door leading into the main hall.

"Where are you going, John?'' asked Lord Sarre.

"Outside! Someone is in trouble!''

"Are you sure, John?'' The viscount's face reflected doubt and concern.

"It isn't one of my deliriums, Tony,'' answered John grimly. "I left off having those when the fevers abated. I assure you, I do hear something!''

Evidently convinced at last, Lord Sarre followed his brother into the hall. While John pulled loose the latch and opened the door, admitting an alarming quantity of blustering rain, Lord Sarre struggled to tug on his boots.

"Shall I wake up the servants, Tony?" asked George. But the question was unnecessary. Finally prodded from slumber, the butler appeared, wishing to know what all the racket was about and if he might be of assistance. Swiftly following on the heel of their superior, other servants crowded into the hallway. Pummelled with questions, the viscount was unaware that John had left the house.

"He's gone, Tony!" George exclaimed.

Without another word, the viscount followed. When the butler and two other servants were required to push the door shut against the wind, George's fears escalated.

"What the deuce is going on?" It was the admiral's gruff baritone, and heartily glad was George to hear it. She was about to explain the situation to him when Jane and the dowager appeared, robes thrown hastily on and hair disheveled. When she had told them all she knew, the admiral took charge, commanding his servants as if they were a ship's crew under siege. Soon several of them were dressed and had gone outside in search of the viscount and Captain Braithwaite.

When George observed how distressed Jane really was, her face pale and her whole frame trembling,

George drew near and caught hold of one of her hands. Squeezing it tightly she whispered, "They'll be all right!"

"But he's so much thinner than he used to be! If it is some sort of vessel in distress, he may try to save some poor wretch from drowning, and in the process..."

"Hush! Captain Braithwaite is too intelligent to expose himself to foolish risks! And Tony is with him! Trust God and their own good sense to bring them safely back!"

"I'll put my trust in God, but as to the other..." exclaimed Jane with a shaky laugh. George smiled her approval of Jane's plucky refusal to succumb to the vapours, but her own heart felt as though it was being squeezed of every drop of blood it possessed. Until this moment she hadn't known how very much Tony meant to her.

LORD SARRE, finding it extremely difficult to walk with any speed or precision against the force of such a wind, struggled to the sands. Blinking through the deluge of water streaming down his face, and with the wind snatching his breath away, he endeavoured to keep the vague outline of his brother's slender shape in view.

Marvelling at the strength John had summoned up for the occasion, Lord Sarre's heart burned with love and respect for his brother's valiant spirit. How could

John have ever supposed he was less of a man because of a lost limb?

Finally he reached the beach and the cries for help were louder. The waves were monstrous in size and thundered into shore with the force of a legion of horses. Only a strip was left of the former wide expanse of sand. The viscount caught up with his brother along this narrow plank between the raging sea and the cliffs that confined them on the other side. If a wave should happen to swallow up the remaining few feet of beach, they would be sucked out to sea with a certainty. Lord Sarre did not fancy a watery grave, but he knew his conscience as surely as John knew his. If people could be saved, it was his duty to help in any way possible.

They each caught sight of the fishing boat at the same moment. It was wedged between the large rocks which jutted a few feet out into the sea. Unable to loose itself, the small vessel was battered again and again by the relentless waves. Lord Sarre knew it was only a matter of time before the entire structure was torn apart and its ragged boards strewn along the shore. The men who clung to its masts knew it too, but though they were only a few yards out, they dared not jump into the water to swim ashore. It seemed inevitable that the sea would have them in the end, but they had no wish to precipitate the matter.

The viscount took stock of the situation, his mind racing over every possibility for rescue. "There's only one solution," he shouted to his brother.

"Yes, I know," John responded. "They're doomed if they remain as they are. They'll have to jump in and try to swim forward with a wave. As it comes ashore, we must snatch them before they're pulled out again!"

By now the servants from the house had arrived on the scene and were looking to the two brothers for guidance.

"It's the only way," agreed the viscount, fixing his brother with a hard stare. "But you must promise to let me do it with the help of these men! You dare not come into the water, John. I forbid it!"

John nodded his head, and Tony could appreciate what a struggle it was for his brother to allow common sense to overrule the stronger urge to participate more fully in the rescue. The plan thus decided upon, they attempted to communicate the procedure to the five men stranded on board the boat with the use of hand signals. At last one of them appeared to understand and to muster up the necessary courage for such a risky manoeuvre. He staggered to the edge of the boat and hovered there, the swirl of the sea undoubtedly more frightening at such close proximity.

The viscount and the captain relayed the plan to the servants just as the first man leapt over the side. Borne to within feet of the shore, he struggled and gasped in the shallow water and would surely have been carried out again by the next wave if the viscount and two of his uncle's footmen had not promptly lurched forward and grasped him by the arms, pulling him to shore.

The rest of the crew took heart at this successful rescue and all of them leapt over the side of the boat at once. It had not occurred to them that rescuing four of them at a time would be extremely difficult, if not impossible.

"Good God!" expostulated the viscount. But all he could do was pitch himself into the water and grab a hand here or a leg there. He'd managed to drag two of the men to safety with the help of one of the stable-lads and had turned to retrieve yet another when a sudden, vicious pain knifed through his brain.

Darkness enveloped him, but as he sank into unconsciousness his mind clung tenaciously to a thought, an image, a promise. . . . *Georgiana.*

CHAPTER NINE

THE AMBER GLOW OF DAWN bathed the wood-strewn beach in a radiant serenity. The storm had raged until the wee hours of the morning, but now the sun reigned supreme, its benevolent face shining on the sea-washed sands. Gulls and every other variety of bird feasted on the fish that had washed ashore. Cawing and chirping excitedly, they ate to repletion, then squabbled with one another for the picked-over bones.

Inside Neptune House the occupants were resting or restless. George made up part of the latter group, her soft kid slippers wearing a hole in the drawing-room carpet. Having spent a perfectly sleepless night, George had allowed Perkins to bully her into changing her gown and sitting still just long enough for her hair to be brushed and tied with an apple-green ribbon. Jane had begged her to take breakfast with Isabella and her mother, but with Tony lying unconscious in his bedchamber with a sober-faced physician in attendance, George found it impossible to eat.

The dowager, the admiral and Jane were allowed inside the sickroom, but as George wasn't related to the viscount, the physician had forbidden her entry. John lay exhausted in his own bed and Jane trod faithfully back and forth between the rooms of her two cousins, overseeing their care and keeping watch on their progress. Occasionally Jane would stop in the drawing-room to speak with George, but in the course of the morning no changes to the viscount's condition had occurred.

As the mantel-clock struck noon, George sank into a wing chair and stared into the banked pile of wood in the fireplace. She had a dim impression of being rather chilly, but she deemed it a selfish motive to call on a servant to light a fire when they were all so busy. The men from the fishing boat, who had all survived thanks to Tony and the captain and the brave servants who'd assisted them, were camped out in a downstairs sitting-room. The fishing boat had set sail from Bleadon in the early morning of the previous day, but on its way back to port had been claimed by the storm and buffeted about capriciously until fixing itself on the rocks. Off and on all morning the families of the men came to carry them home, blessing the sainted gentlemen who'd risked their necks to save the lives of their menfolk, and clucking sadly over the present condition of the viscount.

Whenever George succumbed to self-pity, she reminded herself that Tony could have been dead. After a loosened board from the fishing boat had been hurled at his head by a swell of water, Tony had dropped like a lifeless doll. If the captain had not been willing to put his own life in peril and wrestle a determined under-current for possession of his brother's body, Tony would have been washed out to sea.

"George!"

George jumped up eagerly at the cheerfulness in Jane's voice and they met in the middle of the room. Jane seized both of George's hands and cried, "Tony's awake! He's going to recover! Dr. Holsworthy says he must rest, but Tony's perfectly coherent and remembers everything that happened up until the moment he was hit by the board!"

"Oh, Jane, I'm so happy!" declared George, her eyes brimming with tears of relief and joy.

"I knew you would be! Except for telling John, who's been unable to truly rest while Tony's condition has been at all questionable, I came directly to you. Now, you silly goose, perhaps you'll eat something and rest! You're looking peaked, my dear!"

"Oh, I don't care how I look!" cried George, wiping her eyes with the back of her hand and smiling in so absurd and uncontrollable a fashion she was sure Jane must think her mad.

"I don't know any woman who does not wish to look beautiful for the man who has attached her affection," observed Jane archly.

The smile vanished from George's face. "Oh, Jane, you are quite wrong! Tony and I are friends, only friends!" At least that was how Tony had always described their relationship, thought George. Now that she'd discovered the blissful, painful reality of loving someone, she desired something quite different from him, but she didn't suppose that wishes on her part would change his intentions.

"Why do you so readily assume I'm speaking of Tony?" asked Jane, her eyes alight with mischief.

Since George was thrown into utter confusion by this playful sally, Jane took pity and, giving George an impetuous hug, said, "Well, I'll not quiz you about it, goose! But I daresay that as soon as Dr. Holsworthy has declared Tony fit for company other than his immediate family, he'll be asking for you directly! It would be better if you slept a little and had a cup of tea and a few biscuits at the very least! Do it for me, George!"

George was about to obey meekly, when a sudden impish quirk came over her. "Jane, you tease me, but I could as easily tease you! Your concern for the captain strikes me as rather more than cousinly!"

Jane blushed prettily and George was thankful to observe that the introduction of the subject had not thrown Jane into gloom. The events of last evening had perhaps done *some* good! Pulling George down to sit beside her on the sofa, Jane seemed eager to share confidences.

"George, I can't tell you how much happier I am today than I've been for the past year! Before John was sent to Brussels, we'd entered into a secret engagement! Yes, you may stare! It was wrong of me, but I was so in love with him I couldn't say no!"

"But why did it have to be secret, Jane?" asked George. "Surely your father approved of John."

"He did not disapprove of John, but since the two of us had been close as children, my father wanted me to be sure of my feelings. He didn't want me to confuse a childish affection with the kind of love required for a good marriage. He insisted that I spend a Season in Town with my Aunt Phoebe, where I might meet other men. I knew that there'd be no end of trouble if I refused to go! But John was angry with Father and begged that I commit myself to him before leaving for London. I was perfectly sure that no man could replace John in my heart, whether I was engaged to him or not, but I only agreed to do it with the gravest reluctance! I did not like to hide anything from my father. But if it brought John peace of mind as he set out to war, was it so very wrong of me, George?''

Refusing to answer such a personal question, George prompted, "What then, Jane?"

"We received word of John's accident while I was in the midst of preparing for yet another pointless evening of routs and parties. Along with Tony's letter came a sealed missive for me. It was from John. He was releasing me from my commitment. He said that he knew I'd entered into the engagement most unwillingly. And now, he said, he didn't suppose that any woman should be expected to accept a 'disfigured cripple' for a husband!''

"Oh, Jane! Were those his precise words?" cried George, her ready sympathy deeply stirred.

"I shall never forget them," said Jane quietly. "You cannot imagine the pain I felt for him—and for myself, because I'd lost him! I poured my heart out in letters, but he returned them unopened. When we met on the beach the other day, George, I hadn't seen him since we'd parted as lovers a year ago."

"How horrid for you!" exclaimed George feelingly. "No wonder you've been so unhappy and silent."

"But do not break your tender heart for me, George," exclaimed Jane triumphantly. "I know now that John still loves me! He is talking to me just as he used to do! His looks are open and affectionate! I own my hopes are rising with each moment that passes!"

"To what do you credit this change?" asked George, her own smile reflecting Jane's happiness.

"Perhaps seeing me again has convinced him that my love is constant," mused Jane, a soft, faraway look coming into her hazel eyes. "And perhaps even more to the point, he has confirmed in his own mind that he is still a brave and vigorous man! He'll not beg congratulations for it, mind you, but he's proud to have been the one to save Tony!"

George was about to bring up the subject of Tony's plans to build a seaside resort when the drawing-room door burst open and Micah stomped in, the usual pleasantly vague expression on his face replaced by anger.

"And whose idea was it to exclude me from the goings-on?" he demanded to know, standing stiffly indignant before them.

"Whatever can you mean, Micah?" Then, realizing for the first time that Micah had been absent during the course of last night's drama and during all her anxious waiting of the morning, George exclaimed incredulously, "You don't mean to say that you've just become aware of the mayhem of the last several hours, do you?"

"If Bennett had not casually alluded to it while he brushed my green coat, I should still be ignorant!"

"Have you been abed all this time, Mr. Shelby?" Jane enquired mildly, trying hard to suppress a smile.

"Abed, but not asleep! Even with the curtains drawn round my bed and a pillow over my head, that blasted storm cut into my rest 'til nearly dawn. Managed to drift off then peacefully enough, but I'm peeved beyond anything to have been denied a part in last night's excitement! Could have been helpful, I daresay! Not the least pudding-hearted, y'know! Can't imagine why no one roused me!"

Neither of the ladies had the slightest clue as to why Micah had not been roused to assist in the rescue, except that no one had thought of him. And since they doubted that he would appreciate such an explanation, they remained silent.

At this crucial point, while Micah continued to stare at them, the admiral, Mrs. Lacy, Isabella, the dowager and Doctor Holsworthy entered the room.

"But who is with John and Tony?" asked Jane.

"Linders and John's man—can't recall his name!" answered the admiral. "I suspect my nephews'll be sleeping the greater part of the day. Holsworthy here has given them each a paregoric draught."

The good doctor had been invited into the drawing-room for a glass of brandy. He'd had an exhausting night and was grateful to be able to wet his whistle before returning to his much less sumptuous residence in the village.

"Good God, Jacob!" he exclaimed, collapsing into the chair next to the fireplace. "You'll all be down with the consumption and on a diet of goat's whey if you don't keep a fire in the grate. Chilly in here!"

The admiral pulled the bell-rope and was about to excuse the servants' overlooking the drawing-room grate by alluding to their numerous other duties that day, when Lady Sarre piped up, "You're quite right, Doctor Holsworthy! A shameful neglect! But though I agree with you on *this* point, I must tell you how I feel about the disgraceful habit you physicians have of quacking strong young men with laudanum...."

Mrs. Lacy and Isabella had seated themselves on a distant sofa and were arranging their skirts artfully around them on the cushion. In a rare fit of motherly concern, Mrs. Lacy beckoned George to sit beside her, saying, "You're pale, George. You had better use my rouge pot before dinner. It will not do for Micah to see you so hagged!"

George murmured something incoherent which satisfied her mother and that great lady's composure was left unruffled for the present. Mrs. Lacy's and Isabella's serenity bespoke a night of untroubled sleep, and though they had mouthed dulcet expressions of shock and sympathy over last evening's events, their anxiety was tempered by the certainty that the viscount was hale and hearty and would hardly expire from a mere concussion. But when Lady Sarre continued forcefully to offer her unsolicited opinions to the doctor, their Madonna-like expressions began to melt away.

"That woman is insufferable!" hissed Mrs. Lacy to Isabella. "I fervently hope that once you are married to Lord Sarre, you'll spend a good deal of time in Town. At Aldsworth she would be underfoot incessantly and would likely prove to be the bane of your existence!" Since Mrs. Lacy intended to spend the greater part of the year with her elder daughter, such a dire prediction could be in no way comforting to either of them.

"'Tis just another reason to wish myself married elsewhere, Mama," whined Isabella with one of her famous pouts.

"Isabella!" warned her mother.

"You needn't worry. I said I'd marry him and I shall! But he hasn't asked me, and you've not come up with an idea how he might be compelled to compromise me!"

Mrs. Lacy snatched a quick glance at her younger daughter. George attempted to convince her mother that she hadn't heard Isabella's outburst by assuming a vacuous stare. She hoped she wouldn't be ordered away. In the anxiety of the last few hours, George had forgotten her mother's plot against the viscount, but she was now forcefully reminded of her duty to Tony.

"George," said her mother in buttery accents, "be a dear and fetch my reticule, will you?"

George sighed, stood up and crossed the room to the door. Then, remembering that she hadn't a clue as to where her mother's reticule might be, she turned to ask her where it was. She was startled to observe that her mother, instead of sneering at Lady Sarre's continued lecturing of the doctor, was listening to the discourse with rapt attention.

"It disorients and weakens them!" the dowager was saying.

"It dulls the pain, madam!" insisted the doctor.

"It makes them forgetful and groggy!"

"Then they forget how deuced uncomfortable they are! Please, Lady Sarre, with all due respect, I'm the physician here! I hope Admiral Braithwaite will listen to *me* and continue to dose those two young men throughout the day. Tomorrow if they're feeling up to it, the dose may be reduced or eliminated as they choose. But at present they are both in considerable pain...."

"Pain builds character!" Lady Sarre briskly pointed out.

And so the squabbling continued. Since her mother for once seemed to be entertained by the dowager, George decided not to disturb her. If she had to spend time searching for the reticule, at least it was an excuse to absent herself for a while. With a sudden inspiration, George glanced over at Micah. This was a perfect opportunity to tell him about her mother's plot. He was leaning against the mantelpiece and was still looking piqued over his exclusion from the rescue. She stared at him until he looked at her. She widened her eyes speakingly and jerked her head twice in the direction of the door.

Catching her meaning directly, Micah seemed disinclined to obey her summons. He lowered his eyelids and lifted his nose, the perfect image of wounded sensibilities. Tired, hungry and not in the least inclined to smooth over his lacerated pride, George could feel the wrath building inside her. But knowing from past experience that demanding something of Micah was the surest way to fix his stubborn mind against it, she subdued her mounting ire and threw him a soft, appealing look which begged him to come.

No match for George's "eloquent peepers," as he had been wont to call her blue eyes on occasion, Micah followed her out the door. With the door securely shut behind them, George pulled Micah into a deep window embrasure in the hall. Glancing about to make sure no servants were nearby, she launched into her sordid story, leaving no detail of her mother's and Isabella's conversation untold.

"Good God!" ejaculated Micah, horrified. "I suspected they may try something of this nature at the outset of the trip. But lately I'd begun to hope that Isabella was above this sort of thing."

"She isn't the girl we used to play with, Micah," George reminded him. "Mama has formed Isabella's every thought since she bloomed into a young woman. I can only be thankful I wasn't born the perfect image of my mother or perhaps I should have been compelled to fulfil her girlhood fantasies as well! Now, I fear, Isabella is too hardened in her selfish vanity to know the difference between right and wrong! Mama certainly doesn't!"

Micah's brow had puckered into a deep, dismal frown. "A pity," he observed quietly. Then, with a huge sigh, he said, "Well, since we do not know precisely how the old . . . your mother means to carry out the deed, there's no use in warning Tony. He's too befuddled by the draught to understand anything I might say to him."

"What are we to do?" asked George. Then a sudden painful thought intruded and she blurted out, "Perhaps Tony wouldn't wish to be saved from a marriage to Isabella. Perhaps he means to ask her anyway!"

"You can banish that thought, George!" Micah returned tersely. "Tony does not intend to marry Isabella! Not the man for her anyway, y'know! And even if he did wish to marry her, he would object strenuously to being tricked in such a way!"

George hardly dared believe such a revelation and she stared up into Micah's eyes beseechingly.

"You needn't look at me like that!" he informed her dampeningly. "I'll not tell you anything more!"

"But Micah..." George objected, tugging at his coat sleeve.

Observing that fatigue and anxiety had etched dark circles beneath her eyes, Micah patted her awkwardly on the shoulder and said in a gruff voice, "Don't fret, George. All will be well in the end. By Jupiter, I promise you that!" Then shrugging off her clinging hands, he turned and walked towards the stairs.

"You won't even tell me what you're going to do?" she demanded, abandoning the soft approach and stamping her foot on the floor.

"Trust me!" he said over his shoulder. "And for God's sake, George, go to bed and get some sleep!"

Watching Micah's dandified form ascend the stairs, his carrot-coloured head bowed in deep thought, George hoped she wasn't harbouring a fool's hopes by entrusting Micah with such an important mission.

LORD SARRE DRIFTED through a purgatory of disjointed dreams. Nightmarish visions of waves huge enough to suck a man into swirling tunnels of foam, and to spit him out later on a barren beach, bloated and lifeless, plagued his troubled sleep. Sometimes pleasant phantoms claimed his agitated brain and he saw fields of golden daffodils wafting on the breeze, while a magical creature with golden hair and sapphire eyes danced among the faeries.

He frequently woke from these drug-induced wanderings in a cold sweat, but sometimes with a smile. Linders sat by his bed 'til nearly midnight, but when Lord Sarre woke to find his faithful servant nodding in a chair, he ordered him away. Observing that his master seemed quite testy when he begged to remain, Linders reluctantly removed himself from the room, leaving a candle burning on the mantelshelf so that he might pop his head in to check on the viscount at regular intervals.

Lord Sarre settled back into the downy comfort of his warm bed and endeavoured to steer his dreams towards the fields of daffodils and that fetching golden nymph. He longed for the morrow to come so that he might summon George to see him. He doubted that they'd let him leave his bedchamber, but he'd deuced well refuse any more of that damnable laudanum! Fogged a man's mind! Now where was he...? He prodded his fading consciousness to remember. Ah, yes, Georgiana... He slept.

Was it a dream, or was it real? Had his door creaked open and an illusory flutter of white slipped through the crack? It approached. It floated across the floor in silent, winged slippers. It lighted by the side of his bed and stood over him. He seemed incapable of moving, but his heart beat with a hammering urgency. The curtains to his bed were drawn on one side against the light from the window, and except for the candle on the mantelshelf shining weakly behind this apparition, the room was dark.

"Who is it?" he uttered, his throat dry from the laudanum.

It didn't answer, but a white hand reached out and pulled the covers back. He sensed a hesitation. Then, as if the thing had made a decision, it quickly slipped into bed beside him and lay as still as a mouse.

Was it George come to him? It had to be! She must love him, then! But it was unlike her, for he knew her principles to be high. Therefore he couldn't allow her to give herself to him! Not like this, not without the sanction of matrimony! All must be right and honourable between them from the first. But before he sent her away, before he banished the faerie from his bed, he *must* kiss her! Only once! Once on those dewy, rose-pink lips . . . He reached for her.

But this wasn't George. This full and bosomy figure, these long, straight strands of hair did not belong to George! Oh, good God, it was—

"Isabella!" But the viscount had not said the dreaded name. It was Micah's voice, wrathful and accusing. The drawn curtains of the bed were yanked aside. Moonlight streamed across the covers, illuminating Isabella's frightened face and effectively shocking Lord Sarre into complete consciousness.

"Get out of that bed at once!" Micah ordered, his whole body trembling with anger.

Isabella obeyed him, but instead of scampering away as the viscount expected her to do, she stood shivering by the bedside, her arms crossed protectively against her chest.

"M-Micah," she stammered in a small voice. "What are you d-doing here?"

"I might ask you the same question, Isabella!" he answered tersely.

"You mustn't think I meant to...to...." she quavered.

"To what, Isabella?" Micah spat out deploringly. "No doubt you felt safe crawling into bed with a man who's as weak and harmless as a kitten, quite incapable of ravishing you...."

The viscount thought Micah's expressions rather too strong, but forbore contradicting him.

"...but if Linders found you in bed with the viscount, and Tony was too befuddled by the medicinal draught the doctor had given him to gainsay your story of seduction, he would be honour-bound to marry you whether you had been truly compromised or not! Do I have it right so far? I've been on the watch all night, y'see, and when I saw Linders leave the room I came in and hid myself behind the curtain. I hoped you'd think better of it right up until the moment you crawled into the bed. Gave you every benefit of the doubt, Isabella!"

Isabella's head bowed in shame.

"And which is the greater dishonour?" he continued in a firm, quiet tone. "To have been involved in a commonplace seduction, or part of a loathsome plot involving flagrant dishonesty and blackmail! Knew about it all, y'see. Wished it weren't so, but had to take precautions!''

By now Isabella was crying softly, her hands covering her face. Lord Sarre was surprised to discover the girl had a heart and conscience beneath her vain exterior, and was even more surprised at the powerful authority with which Micah had chastised her.

"Go to your room," Micah ordered her wearily. But as she turned to leave, the door was opened by Linders, still fully clothed and with candle in hand. He seemed about to demand an explanation as to why the viscount was entertaining visitors at such an hour when he got a good look at Isabella. Seeing her standing red-eyed in the middle of the room, with her thin lawn nightgown declaring the object of her visit to be more than ordinary, he could not help but exclaim in a very loud voice, "Upon my word, sir! Mean to say…" Then, observing Micah coming round from the other side of the bed and rapidly approaching, he felt he'd stumbled on something his wildest imaginings could hardly conceive. He'd heard of these sorts of goings-on amongst the Quality, but his lordship had always seemed such a decent young man!

"Close the door, Linders!" said the viscount in a rasping whisper. "You'll have the whole house up!" But Linders was too dumbfounded to move, and it was Micah who extracted the knob from the stunned valet's unresisting grip and shut the door.

"I don't know what to say," the valet muttered, his eyes flickering from one to the other of them.

"You'll say nothing," Micah informed him, removing his jacket and throwing it over Isabella's trembling shoulders. "If one word gets out—" But Micah might as well have saved his breath. The door opened again and people flooded the room. There was Jane, the admiral, Mrs. Lacy and even the dowager. The only one missing was George.

GEORGE HAD SOMEHOW MANAGED to stay awake until her usual bedtime. She'd cherished the hope that she might be allowed to see Tony, but he'd slept all day, just as the admiral had predicted. She fell asleep the moment her head touched the pillow, and George's rest was deep and dreamless. If Linders hadn't bellowed out in sheer amazement when he found Isabella in the viscount's bedchamber, George would doubtless have slept through the night without stirring.

Sitting up with a start, she wasn't sure what it was that had roused her from such a profound slumber. Then, as she listened carefully, the murmuring of voices and the shuffle of slippered feet could be heard in the hallway. Jumping out of her bed, she picked up a blue merino wrap she'd thrown on a chair, thrust her arms into the sleeves and tied it haphazardly at the waist.

She walked swiftly through the moonlit room, threw open the door and perceived at a glance that all the commotion was coming from Tony's room. She could not help but think the very worst: that he'd suffered a relapse and was in grave danger of dying! Her heart beat wildly against her rib-cage as she hurried down the hallway, all the while repeating the same prayer with each breath she drew. Please, he mustn't die! She loved him!

Then, as she burst through the opened door, her eyes flew to Tony's bed. The relief that flooded through her as she perceived him sitting upright against a pillow nearly caused her to swoon. Extending a steadying hand to lean against the wall, she smiled wanly, and said, "Thank God, Tony, I thought..."

She became suddenly aware of the others in the room. There was the admiral, looking grave; Linders was astonished; the dowager seemed consumed with rage; Jane was disgusted; Micah sober and sorry; Mrs. Lacy purple and apoplectic, and Isabella... Good gad, Isabella was in her nightgown! Now it was clear to her. Now all made sense! This was the seduction! This was the compromising situation, and from all appearances her mother and Isabella had pulled the deed off as neat as wax!

They all began to speak at once, producing the most confusing gabble of voices. Nothing in particular they said rose above the general clatter to be understood! She looked at Tony, who, though he was as white as the bandage round his head and appeared slightly dazed, still managed to smile at her. If he could be reduced to an amiable idiot at such a time as this, thought George, he must be stupefied by the lau-

danum! Her heart swelled with indignation. Oh, this
was not fair! This was wrong! She racked her brain
for some way to help him. Finally it came to her. It was
a desperate thing to do, but she must! Summoning up
all her courage she stepped forward and in a very loud
voice, said, "I wish to declare..."

Everyone turned to stare at her. She tucked her wrap
more securely about her and lifted her chin. "I wish to
declare the existence of a previous compromise!"

A deathly silence filled the room. No one spoke, no
one even moved.

"George, you needn't do this!" croaked Tony from
his bed. "There's been no..."

"Don't try to silence me, Tony," she warned him
with a majestic toss of her elfin head. "He—" she
pointed a finger at Tony and looked with wild-eyed
purpose at the others "—he can't marry Isabella!
Lord Sarre compromised me the first day we arrived
in Bleadon! He saw me naked!"

A communal gasp issued from the gaping mouths
of the witnesses, which included, by now, several servants gawking in at the door.

"Oh, George," groaned Tony. "George, George,
George! You goose! There's been no compromise
here! Isabella was caught creeping into my room quite
without my knowledge. Micah saw it all and can vouch
for my total ignorance and lack of participation! I
needn't marry Isabella!" Then, after the exertion of
such a long, heartfelt speech, Tony fell back against
his pillows, exhausted.

George's mouth fell open. "Oh!" was all she managed to say before sinking with rag-doll legs into a nearby chair.

"Georgiana!" began her mother with awful emphasis, her eyes fairly popping from their sockets.

"Never mind her!" interrupted the dowager impatiently. "No doubt *her* compromise was quite unintentional! But that one deserves a licking!" she declared, twitching a spindly finger at Isabella. "In my day, such goings-on weren't tolerated." She grabbed a silver hairbrush from the viscount's dresser top and shook it menacingly in the air.

"If you dare to touch my child," shrieked Mrs. Lacy, "I'll, I'll—"

"You deserve the same treatment, madam," taunted Lady Sarre. "I'll be bound it was you who put the fool idea into the girl's head in the first place! And to have the hypocrisy to fly into a pelter over whatever Miss Georgiana did ought to put you to the blush!"

Mrs. Lacy drew herself up and managed to say with quivering disdain, "Come, Isabella, you'll catch your death!"

"Not before the girl has had her spanking!" declared the dowager, moving purposefully towards Isabella's cowering form.

"Enough is enough, madam!" expostulated the admiral ineffectually, no match for his mother in one of her outraged moods.

"You'll touch this girl over my dead body!" announced Micah, jerking the brush out of the dowager's hand and throwing it onto the bed. "She's not some trollop caught stealing, y'know!" Instead of taking offense at Micah's intervention, Lady Sarre seemed pleased, and with a quizzical little smile, obediently withdrew. "And I'd be much obliged, Admiral," Micah continued, "if you'd remove your gapeseed servants from their vigilant watch at the door, and escort your guests back to their rooms. Isabella's had enough humiliation for tonight, and... and Tony needs his rest!"

"But what about Miss Georgiana?" spluttered the admiral, his sense of order deeply offended by so many loose ends left untied.

George shrank back into the chair as several pair of eyes bore into her.

"Why, Tony'll marry her of course!" Micah said as if the admiral had asked a question to which the answer was self-evident. "But since I'm sure Dr. Holsworthy would deem an affecting betrothal scene too stimulating for his already much stimulated patient, I propose we postpone that business 'til the morrow. Now, if you please..."

Finally the admiral was persuaded to admit the great good sense of all Micah said. He ordered his servants away and bade them, at the risk of losing their positions, to keep all they'd seen within the confines of Neptune House. Everyone else was nudged out the door whether they were willing or not, with the exception of Mrs. Lacy. She was, by now, in the throes of a nervous spasm, leaning heavily on the admiral's reluctantly offered arm, and uttering faint pleas for camphorated spirits of lavender. When she fainted at last, two burly footmen were summoned by the admiral to relieve him of such a tiresome burden, and Mrs. Lacy was borne away to her room with all the dignity of a sack of potatoes.

Perceiving that Isabella's doting mother was incapable of rendering any aid to her favourite child, Micah led Isabella out of the room and down the hall until she could be safely relinquished to Perkins at the door of her bedchamber.

As for George, ever since she'd discovered her confession to be quite unnecessary, she'd been unable to lift her eyes from the gay flowered pattern of the rug covering the bedchamber floor. She dared not look at Tony. While endeavouring to save him from the dreadful expedient of marriage to Isabella for a lesser evil (marriage to her), she'd behaved like a complete fool!

She knew how he felt about being dragged to the altar, and she imagined that he would find being obliged to marry an insignificant Bath chit whom he'd had the misfortune to befriend humiliating indeed!

"Shall I leave you two alone for a moment?" asked Jane, hovering at the door.

"No!" said Tony so emphatically George winced. "From now on I'm a pattern card of respectability!"

George endeavoured to creep out at this point, but was detained by the viscount, who said, "Look at me, George!"

She obeyed and discovered his green eyes kindled and burning brightly. "We'll talk tomorrow," he said, not unkindly, and George was encouraged to hope he would not hate her for making such a shocking muddle of his life. She nodded her head and left the room.

CHAPTER TEN

"WAKE UP, GEORGE! Do you hear me, little sister? I need your help!" The imperious command finally penetrated George's deep slumber and she awoke to find Isabella leaning over her. Her long, chestnut hair fell loosely over one shoulder and she was pressing the front of her dress against her chest as if it were unfastened in the back.

"What's the matter, Isabella? What time is it?" George blinked against the flood of sunshine pouring into her room from the opened draperies. She sat up and rubbed her eyes, striving to focus her bleary gaze on the mantelshelf clock.

"It's just past six o'clock, if you must know!" hissed Isabella impatiently. "And I'm late! But I can't get this dress buttoned and I dare not call Perkins!"

George was jerked into full lucidity by these revelations. Utterly amazed to discover Isabella out of her bed at such an early hour and attempting to dress herself, George knew with a dreadful certainty that something unusual was about to happen. "Good God, you're not running away, are you?" she blurted out.

"No! Nothing of the sort!" retorted Isabella scornfully. "But I shan't tell you precisely what I *am* doing! None of your business, really!"

"If you want my assistance you'll empty your budget now!" George mulishly informed her, raising her brows and crossing her arms across her chest in a stubborn gesture.

"Oh, very well!" said Isabella, turning her back to George. "But fasten me up, if you please, while I tell you! I'm late and I don't want him to go away!"

George had got out of bed and was in the process of buttoning Isabella's gown, but her nimble fingers froze in the midst of the task when Isabella's words sank in. Turning her sister to face her, George said, "Who is *he,* Isabella?"

"Micah," she replied quietly and averted her face. "Last night he made me promise to meet him this morning at six o'clock in that little wilderness at the south end of the garden." She turned to look at George, her eyes suddenly filled with pleading and some other emotion her sister couldn't quite peg. "But it's already ten minutes past the hour! I didn't think it would take so long to dress without Perkins to help me, and I'm afraid he'll go away if I don't hurry, so *please ... !*"

George obediently finished the job, all kinds of intriguing possibilities teasing her mind as to why Micah wished for a secret rendezvous with her sister. If she'd been told a week ago that Micah had willingly sought an audience with Isabella, she'd have dismissed the idea as ludicrous. Isabella always treated him so shabbily he'd have to be an absolute slow-top to provide her with another opportunity to abuse him. But even more incredible was Isabella's obvious desire to go. Her exertions of the morning were quite out of character and George's amazement was only equalled by her burning curiosity to know all.

Isabella now stood before the mirror, smoothing her dress with trembling fingers and biting her bottom lip until it looked ready to bleed.

"Calm down, Isabella!" George admonished her. "'Tis only Micah! He'll not eat you!"

"But my hair . . . ! It's a mess!" she wailed.

"My dear sister, you amaze me!" George said, taking a brush from the dressing-table and smoothing Isabella's tangled hair. "I'm surprised to see you going to so much trouble for someone you've frequently described as a positive mushroom!"

"Oh, I'll never say such a thing again as long as I live!" declared Isabella passionately. "He's been so kind!" Her voice broke and she dropped her head to stare at the smooth cherrywood finish of the dressing-table and fidget abstractedly with the silver-filigreed comb lying there. "I've behaved abominably!" she blurted out at last.

"Well," observed George matter-of-factly, "I daresay you listened to Mama more than you ought!"

Isabella sniffed meekly in reply.

Encouraged by this sign of repentance, George tactfully continued. "I know she loves you and wishes you to be comfortably established, but sometimes her methods are . . . Well, they're not precisely . . .''

"Oh, you needn't beat about the bush, George! I know she's been quite wrong, and . . . and *I've* been wrong, too!"

This statement was unanswerable, and it swelled George's heart with hope that Isabella meant to reform! She knew better than to belabour the point with righteous moralizing, however, and said nothing more.

Eventually George decided that the poignant pause had run its course and she ventured to say, "If you're worried that Micah means to ring a peal over you this morning, you needn't fret. He's not like that. Besides, you're not the only one of us in need of a rare trimming," she added ruefully.

"Oh! Yes, I've been meaning to ask you, George," began Isabella as she turned around, her eyes alight with speculation. "How on *earth* did the viscount contrive to see you—"

"Not now!" George cut her off, unequal to a hasty explanation. "You're late, remember?"

Isabella acknowledged the truth of this, resumed her fidgeting as before, and moved hesitantly to the door. Then, with her hand on the knob, she turned with a most imploring look and said, "Come with me, George!"

"But I'm not even dressed," George objected, "and you're late already."

Isabella did not reply, only looked as pathetic as possible. George gave up. "Oh, all right," she said with an exasperated gurgle of laughter. Isabella smiled her gratitude, while George dressed herself as rapidly as possible and ruthlessly dragged a comb through her hair.

They managed to exit the house without meeting anyone and quickly found themselves approaching the copse of trees that Micah had indicated. It appeared that Micah had worn his favourite powder-blue coat for the occasion, because George could see the colour peeping through the branches as he paced back and forth.

"I'd better leave you here, Isabella," George whispered. "I'm sure Micah wants to see you alone, or he wouldn't have chosen such an early hour of the day to meet you."

Isabella gripped George's arm. "But I'm frightened!"

"Of what?" reasoned George.

"Perhaps he means to spank me this morning," she suggested, her eyes wide with horror. "He would not do so last night in front of everyone, but who's to say he wouldn't do it now?"

Her eyes twinkling irreverently, George was about to observe that a spanking was not totally uncalled for, but she decided that Isabella would not appreciate such an opinion. Instead she said, "Oh, I don't think so! But if you insist on dragging me with you, you just *may* find Micah a trifle out of patience!"

"I don't care! He'd no right ordering me out here in the first place," Isabella declared with a petulant droop to her pretty mouth. "If the servants should happen to see us, there's no telling what they might construe from my meeting him alone!"

"I hardly think *that* much of a consideration after last night," George said, laughing. "Don't be a goose! You might as well stop making up excuses to dally here! Now's not the time to cry craven!"

But they'd stood talking long enough to have alerted Micah to their presence. Ducking beneath the branches of the trees, he walked towards them.

"What's the idea leaving me to kick my heels, Isabella?" was his charming greeting. Then, glaring at George, he expostulated, "And why the deuce did you bring *her?*"

"A nice way to proceed, Micah," observed George repressively. "Insulting me and cowing Isabella!"

"Well, I wanted to talk to Isabella alone," he explained impatiently, eyeing Isabella's flushed and downcast face with misgiving. "Been worried she wouldn't come! Didn't mean to fly into the boughs! Beg your pardon, Isabella!"

Isabella's head reared up and her eyes flew to Micah's face. "Oh no, don't beg *my* pardon. It is *I* who should beg forgiveness of *you!* I've treated you abominably and held you so cheaply these last few years! But I never imagined you would return these insults with so much kindness!"

Micah's face turned as red as his hair. "Never gave up on you completely," he choked out. "Couldn't forget the sweet, darling girl you used to be!"

George's memory might have been in error, but she couldn't dredge up a single episode from their childhood to support Micah's view of Isabella as a sweet, darling girl. She'd been amiable enough for a spoilt, indulged child, but she'd had temper tantrums even then. Micah was obviously seeing Isabella through rose-coloured spectacles. More to the point, he was in love with her!

Now that George thought about it, she *did* recall something happening the summer just before Micah was sent off to Eton. Isabella was still in pigtails and Micah's voice was the broken sing-song of adolescence. Once, during this idyllic summer, she'd caught them kissing behind the hothouse. Deeply offended by her friend's unmanly behaviour, she'd run in and tattled to the governess, Miss Renshaw. Old Hatchet-Face then proceeded to inform Mrs. Lacy of the misdemeanour and Isabella was kept under strict surveillance until Micah left for school.

No wonder Mrs. Lacy had talked Isabella into disliking Micah over the years, thought George. An early tendre had been nipped in the bud!

"Are you coming, George?"

Micah was leading Isabella into the copse, but Isabella hung back.

"Surely you don't still want *me?*" George responded wonderingly.

"Well, *I* don't!," was Micah's flat reply.

"But, Micah!" Isabella demurred.

"Don't need a chaperon. Mean to keep you only a minute, Isabella, and have you back to your room before Perkins is any the wiser! Only need to tell you one thing!"

"Which is?" Isabella quavered, her eyes fixed on his face and brimming with apprehension.

Micah paused briefly; then, as if he'd decided to throw all caution to the wind, ardently declared, "That I love you, you delectable shrew, and mean to marry you! Will you have me?"

Isabella's gasp could be construed in no other way than as a positive yes. Enraptured by her expression, Micah leant over to kiss her. But remembering just in time that they were not alone, he turned to prod George out of her state of bemusement.

"Know you're the curious sort, George," Micah observed with asperity. "But some things are meant to be private, y'know!"

Finding it impossible to wrench her eyes from Isabella's adoring countenance, George became aware that her feet seemed to have taken root.

"Do go away, George!" Micah shouted at last, past patience and obviously wishing to consummate his betrothal with something more intimate than a handshake.

Recalled with a jerk to reality, George turned away as Micah escorted Isabella into the copse. George dared not imagine how her mother would react to the news of her elder daughter's betrothal. It was hardly the brilliant match she'd hoped for. But George couldn't be more pleased. Somehow she knew that however difficult the task, Micah would relish taming his "delectable shrew," and make the shrew happy as well. Now if only she could feel as positive about her own situation!

Last night, after leaving Tony's bedchamber, she'd tumbled into bed and indulged a crying fit that lasted a good ten minutes. Then, roundly declaring herself a silly watering-pot, she dried her tears with the edge of the sheet and grimly resolved to make things right on the morrow. She would explain everything to the others: how the viscount hadn't actually seen her totally naked and how it had all been an innocent accident. Since Jane had witnessed the whole thing, she would no doubt support her in exoncrating Tony from any suspicion of wrongdoing. Having decided on a course of action, she fell asleep instantly.

Now George began to have doubts. Tony had originally tried to keep the sea-bathing episode a secret because he mistrusted Mrs. Lacy, and who could be sure her mother wouldn't use the circumstance even now to force Tony to marry her? *Especially* now, since her hopes for Isabella had been dashed, it was completely possible that Mrs. Lacy's practical side would rear its ugly head and she'd decide to use her younger daughter to fulfil her loathsome ambitions. This daunting possibility was lowering, and George's spirits sank.

She entered the house and ran quickly up the stairs to her room, where she sat in a thoughtful, brooding state until Perkins interrupted her. The abigail briskly bid her a good morning, laid out a rose-pink muslin gown and brushed George's hair into a becoming pompadour of curls. And even though Perkins did all this without gawking curiously at her, as George had fully expected her to do, George was not cheered up.

For a brief moment she wished fervently to be relieved of all her principles. If her whole heart and soul did not recoil so vehemently from the idea of marrying Tony against his will, the deed could be done in a trice. He was an honourable man, and given the fact that she'd announced to the household that he'd seen her naked, there was no doubt in her mind he meant to make her an offer of marriage. Tears welled in her eyes. Such a declaration was what she wished to hear from Tony above all things, but not under duress!

"Perkins, how is my mother this morning?" George asked the servant at last, contemplating the possibility of confronting her mother while she was still overcome by last night and refusing to be involved in a forced marriage to the viscount.

"Very poorly, miss," replied Perkins in a disapproving voice. "She'll not be awake until this afternoon, I can tell you for a certainty. Quacked herself with a large dose of laudanum, and to no good purpose!" She clucked her tongue and shook her head. "She'll have to face up to last night's work sooner or later, and it might as well be sooner!"

George was thankful the servant hadn't mentioned her own shameful revelation of the night before and longed to explain it to her. But she decided that she'd better save her energy for the others, and knew, at any rate, that whatever she told the admiral's household of relatives and guests would quickly become common knowledge in the servants' quarters. She contented herself with smiling gratefully at the abigail, then asked, "Have you seen Isabella yet this morning, Perkins?" She fixed her gaze on the servant to observe any change in her countenance.

"I went to her room before coming here, miss," Perkins answered, with a rather puzzled frown creasing her forehead. "She was up, which much surprised me, and was sitting at the dressing-table in a sort of daze. I expected her to look red-eyed and hagged this morning, but she was the picture of blooming beauty! And smiling into the bargain! After last night, I was never so surprised in my life!"

"Did she explain her recovery?" George asked cautiously, hoping Isabella had not been so unwise as to confide in her abigail before properly preparing her mother for the blow.

"No. She merely sent me away! Said she wasn't ready to be dressed, then fell to gathering wool again." Perkins leaned closer to George and said in a low, ominous whisper, "I hope she hasn't lost her wits over this business!"

Whether Isabella had lost her wits or not would no doubt be debated at length once news of her betrothal was out, thought George with amusement. But to

Perkins she only said in a bracing tone, "Don't worry about her. She'll be fine!"

When Perkins had gone, George was trying to decide what to do next. Perhaps while her mother slept she could call a meeting of sorts with the others and explain about the sea bath. Then, when her mother awoke, any plans she had to force Tony's hand would be thrown out when she observed that no one supported her. Itching to do *something*, George braced herself for the embarrassment of facing the others with her foolish admissions.

She left her bedchamber and descended the stairs, turning at the bottom in the direction of the breakfast room. She'd probably find several of the others eating breakfast by now and discussing her infamous family with a vengeance. She could just imagine how silent the room would become the moment she entered it.

"Miss Lacy?" Linders approached her from the opposite end of the hallway. Recalling the shocked look on his face last night when she'd declared the existence of a previous compromise, George blushed furiously. But this morning Linders was as calm and collected as could be. Neither he, nor Perkins for that matter, had shown the least sign of repugnance towards her company. And no matter how well trained a servant was, it was impossible not to be aware of it when one disapproved of you.

"Yes, Linders?" George said nervously.

"Lord Sarre wishes to see you in the library," he politely informed her.

"N-now? But I thought he was too sick to be brought down from his bedchamber! Surely 'tis foolish for him to be up so soon?" blurted George, alarm for Tony's safety quickly replacing any anxiety she felt for herself at being summoned to his presence so peremptorily.

"I agree entirely, miss," said Linders with a pained expression. "But, begging your pardon, miss, there never was a more rock-headed gentleman than his lordship! He's been up since sunrise and for the last hour has had one visitor after the other summoned to his side."

"Good God, what for?" ejaculated George, her imagination running wild at the possibilities.

But Linders knew his limits, and was aware that he'd probably overstepped them already. "I expect his lordship would be the best person to explain himself. Will you come this way, please?"

George knew very well where the library was, but walked timidly behind the poker-backed manservant, as all the while her mind raced, her pulse beat and her hands twisted nervously in front of her.

Linders opened the door and announced her presence in his best stentorian tones. She stepped inside and heard the door close behind her with a sinking heart.

"Come here, George!" ordered the viscount from a settee by the fire, facing away from the door. Because of the position of the settee, he'd been looking in altogether the other direction when she'd entered, and unless he possessed powers beyond human abilities, he couldn't possibly turn his neck far enough around to look at her. But he did turn his head as far as he could, and as George crossed the room she was provided with the opportunity to examine his noble profile without the added perturbation of meeting his gaze.

The bandage was wound round his head, but instead of rendering him pathetic it seemed to add to his attractiveness, lending him a dangerous, romantic air. His black hair fell in waves over the front of the bandage, skimming his vulcan-like brows. She admired his aquiline nose and well-formed mouth, only wishing it were not so firmly compressed! His eyelids drooped languidly, but she suspected that he wasn't in the least bored or sleepy. Finally she stood in front of him and he raised his eyes to hers. George had never seen the emerald-green colour of them so brilliant as now.

"Sit down, child," the viscount said, smiling faintly. George sat in a chair opposite him and observed that he was in a reclining position, but with only one leg stretched out on the cushions and the other resting on the floor. He was booted and dressed in elegant morning wear, and except for the bandage about his head and the blanket thrown over his lap, no one would have suspected he was convalescing.

"Are you sure you should be downstairs, sir?" George ventured to ask.

"We're back to 'sir,' are we? What happened to the confiding child that used to call me 'Tony'?" the viscount demanded, one black brow winging upwards.

Overcome with confusion, George stammered, "She...she behaved stupidly last night and is...is gone forever, I should think, sir!"

"Good God, I hope not!" Lord Sarre declared passionately.

"How can you say so, Tony...I mean...sir!" objected George, her eyes fixed on the carpet. "Hoping to save you from an...an unfortunate marriage to Isabella..."

"'Unfortunate' is too mild a word, Georgiana!"

"I sullied your reputation in front of all your family and all the servants...."

"Impossible to do, you know. Over the years I've conditioned them to be enured against shock where I'm concerned!"

"...and made them all suppose you owed me some kind of declaration! But I mean to tell them the truth! Explain everything! How it was only an accident and..."

"No need, George. I've told them already!"

"...then you will be free to choose whom you wish to marry! As you've said yourself, sir, no one should be dragged to the altar!" Finally perceiving that the viscount had said something of import, her eyes flew to his face. She said, "I beg your pardon, sir? What did you say?"

"I said I've told them already, George," he stated matter-of-factly. "And I charged Linders with the chore of spreading the truth amongst the servants. He was only too happy to do so, having been violently distressed by my presumed wickedness after last night's fiasco! He was pleased to be able to untarnish my reputation, and yours! I may be reprehensible in many respects, Georgiana, but I've never sunk so low as to deflower a daisy with the morning dew still fresh on its petals! Only your mother and Isabella are left in the dark as to the true state of affairs...." His mouth curved in a devilish smile as he added, "If you'll forgive the pun!"

Something about his rakish grin twisted George's stomach into little knots of yearning. Blushing hotly, she said, "Oh! Well, I'm happy to know you've told them the truth! Now we needn't get married!" The desire to throw herself into his arms increasing with the painful knowledge that he'd never be compelled to put them around her, even in the sham of a forced marriage, she weakly added, "I'm so...so glad! Now that that's all settled I expect we shall be going back to Bath as soon as possible!"

The viscount sobered considerably. All trace of mockery or amusement vanished from his face. He studied her silently for a time, and she endured it, relishing the burning intensity of his eyes for what she feared would be the last time!

"I take it you're still as opposed to marriage as you were when we first met, then," he said at last.

"No! I mean yes! Yes, if it's a forced marriage, or a loveless one, forged with regard only to money or social standing! But when two people love each other..." Her voice broke. She dared not speak further about love while her heart was breaking!

The viscount threw the blanket from his lap, swung his leg onto the floor and leant over, clasping his hands together in front of him. In a gentle, penetrating voice, he asked, "Do you still believe that a friend is better than a husband, George?"

She considered this for a long moment, her eyes resolutely fixed upon the carpet again—it was so much safer than looking into his eyes! "Good friends are so pleasant, so comforting.... If only a husband, a l-lover could be a friend, too," she observed pensively. "That would be heaven, indeed!"

"Then heaven awaits us, Georgiana," said the viscount with quiet conviction, lifting her chin with an outstretched hand and earnestly looking into her eyes.

"What can you mean, Tony?" George quavered, her whole body thrown into exquisite torture by the mere touch of his hand. "You can't mean that you wish to marry me, can you?"

"That's precisely what I mean, Georgiana!"

She turned her head, hoping he'd remove the burning, confusing pressure of his fingers against her skin. But instead of pulling away, he moved his hand in a slow and deliberate caress down the side of her neck.

"So soft," he murmured, leaning closer still.

"But I simply can't allow you to marry me out of pity, Tony! You've no reason to marry me now! No doubt there may be some gossip leaking out, but none to signify!"

"Yes, I made sure of that! No one doubts your innocence, George. You're right; now there's absolutely no reason in the world that I should marry you, except one...."

"Oh?" George whispered hoarsely, her throat grown suddenly dry as his magic fingers continued to reduce her to a sweet, delicious state of idiocy.

"I love you, you elfish vixen!"

"You don't!" cried George, sure she was asleep and dreaming.

"How might I convince you of it, faithless one?" he enquired, the kindled fire of his green eyes glinting beneath the seductive droop of his eyelids.

"Perhaps if you k-kissed me, Tony," she ventured to suggest, appalled at her own brazenness. "Then, if I do not find it odious, as I did with Jason Bromley... Or rather, if I found it pleasant, you know..."

Kindly rescuing her from further blitherings, the viscount kissed her. Every nerve in George's body seemed to leap and writhe with pleasure at the simple touch of his lips upon hers. Then, when she began to feel positively weak, he pulled her to her feet, clutched her to his chest and kissed her even more thoroughly than before.

Released at last from such a blissful purgatory, George found herself sitting on Lord Sarre's lap.

"Oh! Somehow I think you *must* love me, Tony," she observed, her lips throbbing and her heart beating wildly. Then, gazing up into his brilliant green eyes and flushed face, she added, "And I must love you, too, for I'd never describe that kiss as odious! No, indeed!"

"Nymph!" declared the viscount with ardour, pinching her cheek. Then he kissed her again.

JANE AND JOHN WERE THE FIRST to marry. It was a quiet ceremony in Bleadon with only family and close friends in attendance. Declining a honeymoon abroad, they took up immediate residence in Neptune House until their own home could be built on the down.

John met Mr. Wood and entered into the resort business with intense enthusiasm, coming home each night to regale his adored and adoring Jane with his latest ideas for the project.

Micah met his magnificent Isabella at the altar in Saint Mary's Chapel in Bath. Though Micah was only of a height with her, Isabella thought he more than made up for his lack of stature with his many excellent traits of character, and, of course, a discreetly elevated heel on his shoe. During the course of their two-month engagement, he had managed to claim the attention of his preoccupied father-in-law long enough to win his respect, and if he did not exactly endear himself to Mrs. Lacy (who took to her bed for three days upon the news of his betrothal to Isabella), he had at least taught her to keep her tongue between her teeth. This he accomplished by threatening to exclude her from the London town house he'd purchased with the help of his father.

Though Micah was only a younger son, with Isabella's considerable dowry their combined income was very comfortable. He hadn't any need to toil for a living, but he'd decided against complete dissipation and busied himself with promotion of the Braithwaite's seaside resort by praising it everywhere he went. At the same time, he escorted his beautiful wife (and her persistently present mother) about Town.

As for Isabella, it would be a fairy tale to say she changed overnight from a self-indulgent, spoilt woman-child into all that was most endearing. She was still prone to exhibit a thoughtless tongue and to make sulky demands, and still tried Micah's forebearance at times.

Despite the ups and downs of their relationship, it was obvious they loved each other and Micah drew many an admiring glance from fellow club members at White's on the nights he managed to drag himself away from his buxom bride. Rumours began to abound that red-haired men had a mysterious virility that other less colourfully thatched men could only wish for. Soon his habit of blinking was attributed to too many late nights in the arms of his ecstatic bride.

The wedding of Lord Sarre to the unknown but charming ingenue, Miss Georgiana Feona Lacy, was the social event of the summer, drawing even the most fashionable to Town during the unfashionable month of August. St. James was full to overflowing, the Braithwaite dynasty proving to be prodigiously large and occupying nearly a fourth of the pews. The admiral recognized only half of those introduced to him as cousins and muttered beneath his breath about "dirty dishes and the shabby genteel."

The dowager beamed beneficently upon the viscount and his new viscountess and proceeded to advise them on rites of fertility and the efficacy of oysters for endurance at the opened door of their coach as they set out from the church. Her grandson firmly informed her that he'd no need of such instructions and closed the door. The dowager accepted this set-down with a satisfied smile, assured them she would take care of Whiskers very properly in their absence, and waved them happily away.

A villa in the south of France with a private beach where one might bathe without the inhibiting confinement of bathing clothes was to be their final destination, but their wedding night would be spent in the viscount's luxurious town house in Grosvenor Square.

George had changed from her wedding gown into an emerald-green day dress and an elegant poke bonnet with a perky green feather curling over the rim, and the viscount found it difficult to look at anyone or anything else.

At the town house, he introduced his wife to the staff, but insisted upon giving her the grand tour without their assistance. The tour completed, they paused outside her bedchamber. He meant to leave her so she could dress for dinner, but was suddenly inspired to comment on the fetching colour of her gown.

"I chose it because it's the exact shade of your eyes," she demurely informed him, moving easily into his welcoming embrace.

"Makes you look more than ever like a leprechaun, you know," observed the viscount, tucking a wayward yellow curl behind her ear. "Where's that pot of gold you elves profess to own?" he demanded, his eyes glinting provocatively. "Now that I've caught you, George, it's only my due!"

George dimpled and blushed. Then, reaching for the doorknob, she stepped inside her bedchamber, saying, "It's in here, Tony!"

With a delighted shout of laughter Tony followed her inside and shut the door.

Observing this touching tableau from the stair landing, Linders strode to the kitchen with the air of a superior servant possessed of privileged information and advised Cook to take the pheasants off the spits. If dinner wasn't late tonight, he was a monkey's uncle!

Harlequin Regency Romance ™

COMING NEXT MONTH

#45 THE WILLFUL LADY by Eva Rutland
Miss Amelia Allen thought her troubles were over
when she inherited a modest fortune from her recently
deceased uncle. She was quickly to learn that her
troubles had only just begun when Guy Grosvenor,
the Duke of Winston, had been appointed her trustee.
The insufferable peacock had previously made it plain
as a pikestaff that he would have her for his mistress
and Amelia had long since decided that she would
rather turn up her toes than submit to such an
odious fate!

#46 LADY ELMIRA'S EMERALD by Winifred Witton
Viscount Oakfort had been cooling his heels in
London waiting for his childhood sweetheart, Lady
Imogen Remlow, to come of age. He had always
assumed they would be married and was quite
unprepared for her rejection. It seemed she had
become betrothed to a poet, more romantic than
Byron, compared to whom George was a dull dog.
But when Imogen loses the emerald pendant
belonging to the viscount's mother, she is soon to
learn that George is anything but dull and she must
cudgel her brains for a way to win his affections
once more.

H A R L E Q U I N
American Romance®

RELIVE THE MEMORIES...

From New York's immigrant experience to the Great Quake of 1906. From the Western Front of World War I to the Roaring Twenties. From the indomitable spirit of the thirties to the home front of the Fabulous Forties. From the baby boom fifties to the Woodstock Nation sixties... **A CENTURY OF AMERICAN ROMANCE** takes you on a nostalgic journey through the twentieth century.

Revel in the romance of a time gone by... and sneak a peek at romance in a exciting future.

Watch for all the **A CENTURY OF AMERICAN ROMANCE** titles coming to you one per month over the next three months in Harlequin American Romance.

Don't miss February's **A CENTURY OF AMERICAN ROMANCE** title, #377—TILL THE END OF TIME by Elise Title.

A CENTURY OF
AMERICAN ROMANCE
1970s

The women...the men...the passions...the memories...

HARLEQUIN

Romance

This March, travel to Australia with Harlequin Romance's FIRST CLASS title #3110 FAIR TRIAL by Elizabeth Duke.

They came from two different worlds.

Although she'd grown up with a privileged background, Australian lawyer Tanya Barrington had worked hard to gain her qualifications and establish a successful career.

It was unfortunate that she and arrogant barrister Simon Devlin had to work together on a case. He had no time for wealthy socialites, he quickly informed her. Or for women who didn't feel at home in the bush where he lived at every available opportunity. And where he had Tanya meet him to discuss the case.

Their clashes were inevitable—but their attractions to each other was certainly undeniable....